**Birmingham City Council**

Loans are up to 28 days. Fines are charged if items
are not returned by the due date.  Items can be renewed
at the Library, via the internet or by telephone up to
3 times. Items in demand will not be renewed.

**Please use a bookmark.**

www.birmingham.gov.uk/libraries
www.birmingham.gov.uk/libcat

# The Gun Hand

Johnny Royal had lived on his wits and his gun ever since he'd left home following a foolish argument. Years later he was heading back, wary of the welcome a prodigal son could expect from hard working, honest parents – until the shooting started.

Young Mariella needed his protection, and that decision was confirmed once he met the beautiful local rancher, Sarah. Rustlers and outlaws had dominated the neighbourhood since Sarah's powerful grandfather had been taken ill, and an old crime masterminded by her uncle had returned to haunt them. Aided by the grizzled old ranch foreman and Sarah, Johnny began to blaze a path of destruction through the forces set against them, searching for her uncle's ill-gotten gains in the teeth of the outlaw's meanest gunslingers.

# The Gun Hand

## ROBERT ANDERSON

**A Black Horse Western**

ROBERT HALE · LONDON

ISBN 978-0-7090-8694-9

Robert Hale Limited
Clerkenwell House
Clerkenwell Green
London EC1R 0HT

www.halebooks.com

Typeset by
Derek Doyle & Associates, Shaw Heath
Printed and bound in Great Britain by
CPI Antony Rowe, Wiltshire

*For Anna*
*Thank you for your enduring love*

# CHAPTER ONE

# A SUDDEN AMBUSH

Johnny Royal allowed his mind to wander while his horse picked its own way through the jumble of rocky outcrops that marked the line of the trail leading down the bluffs to the flat prairie he'd spied from higher up the cordillera. The grass in the far off valley had appeared particularly plump and green from above, a promise of water and also of habitation. From what sparse knowledge of the area he'd garnered the last time he'd met with another human being some two or three days back at the railhead, there was even a small town in the neighbourhood. Boulder, they called it, named, apparently, for the vast piles of stone fringing the shallow stream that ran through its outskirts.

He pulled out a well-thumbed letter from his shirt pocket and began to study it as he'd done so many times before. It was a missive he'd read again and again until he knew the contents by rote, but still he read the words verbatim off the dog-eared paper, speaking them aloud as though they'd make more sense that way. If such a letter could make sense to a man of his sort.

It was an epistle from his father, whom he'd neither seen nor heard from in nigh on twenty years, ever since he'd left on his first disastrous adventure in direct defiance of his pa's instructions. He'd been no more than seventeen years old at the time, and coming into increasing conflict with what he saw as the praetorian demands of his strict forebear. The inevitable had happened, an argument in which both sides had said more than they meant to and, throbbing with righteous indignation, he'd walked out on his home and family, heading for the far-off Californian goldfields where he'd intended to make his fortune.

And now, so many years later, his parents had somehow tracked him down and sent him the letter. In brief, the missive contained a plea for him to return home and take over the running of the ranch. His father was getting too old for the task and needed him in place as his successor; Ma, too, still missed him. That last piece of information had surprised a tear into his eyes the first time he'd read it, but by now he was far too hardened to the contents for it to register with such high emotion.

Did he want to return home? It had taken him six months to take the decision. He'd yearned to return to the ranch so many times since he first set out on his own, but years of rough and dangerous trails had hardened his heart, or maybe he'd just forgotten his filial duties in the difficult job of just staying alive. Those first few years he hadn't returned to the fold purely and simply because he intended to do so only when he was a success; and later he'd stayed away from a knowledge of his own failure and the shame it engendered. His had been a grand failure to make anything of himself, unlike the success his grandpa had made when he first headed west with far less to his credit. Shame of the drifter he'd become: forking cattle for others more fortunate or more deserving; selling his services as a gunman to the highest bidder; gambling and drinking, often enough in the lowest and meanest dens of iniquity.

He'd killed too, both in defence of his own person and in pursuit of his current contract. True he'd never resorted to outright murder, but he knew that in one or two jobs he'd sailed close enough to the wind to make any honest man or woman stare, let alone his virtuous parents. Until the letter had been delivered and stirred his memory, many years had passed since he'd even considered returning home. Now he was on the trail, but would he stay on it? He'd turned back twice already, abandoning the journey in despair, but each time taking it up again after agonizing searches through his heart. Truth was, he desperately wanted to see his ma and pa again, at least once before he died, but he was afraid they wouldn't wish to acknowledge the son he'd become. When he'd started out with all the callowness of youth, he'd convinced himself it was their strictures that started him drifting, but over the years he'd come to see much of the fault lay in his own restless nature.

The sharp crack of a rifle took him by surprise, but years of living on the edge had sharpened his wits and hazy recollections of home fled his brain abruptly while he tumbled out of his saddle and rolled lithely into the nearest semblance of cover. Some prescient sixth sense told him the shot came from the direction of the bluffs, a steep jumble of porous, crumbling rock through which occasional outcrops of the underlying granite protruded. He'd heard the shell whistle through the air somewhere above his head, a near miss certainly, but just how close it had come he really had no idea. Perhaps it had been a mere warning?

The second shot ricocheted noisily off the boulder he'd chosen to shelter himself under and he squirmed closer into its protective bulk, realizing he was being targeted rather than warned. Whoever was shooting at him was no marksman, but had chosen a near perfect spot for an ambush. One man acting on his own, he concluded; the shots were too well spaced for there to be any doubt of that. But why should anyone choose to waylay him? About the only thing he owned of any value was the horse, and that was as travel-worn as himself. He peered around carefully, surveying his position without relish.

His cover was almost non-existent, and it would only require his attacker to shift position by a few yards to leave him exposed once more. Defenceless too. The handgun nestling within the oiled leather holster carried low on one hip would be virtually useless at this range, and it was the only weapon he had available to defend himself with. His mount, carrying a rifle in its protective scabbard, though no more than a dozen yards away, was acting skittish, and there was no telling whether a lightning dart in its direction would cause it to flee and leave him in the open, easy prey to his assailant's fire. The third shot, which hit the boulder that sheltered him with a heavy thud, made up his mind. The horse, already alarmed, cut and ran.

Three well spaced shots. Instinct told him he was dealing with a man handling a single shot weapon and, moreover, one who was not well versed in using it. Why the devil should such a person launch an attack on a chance passer-by? And chance passer-by was what he must be! He'd amassed plenty of enemies over the years, but even supposing they'd managed to track him down, no paid assassin, or even thief, would use such a weapon unless they could reload with far more facility than his present opponent displayed.

With this at the forefront of his mind, he took his life in his hands and flung himself across the open trail to dive head first into the rocks under the bluffs before his assailant was in a position to shoot again. To his relief, he was correct in his suspicions. Not only hadn't he been shot at, but he had the strangest premonition his attacker hadn't even seen him shift his position. Be that as it may, several minutes later the bushwhacker still hadn't fired again, evidently realizing his quarry was no longer pinned down under the dubious cover of an isolated boulder, but unable to detect his new hiding place. Eventually Johnny was driven to snap off a shot of his own, more to convince the man of his ability to defend himself than in any real hope of hitting his target. Not that he'd gotten sight of anyone to shoot at thus far.

His unknown assailant didn't return the shot and, knowing his cover was good, Johnny began to work his way higher up the cliff, drifting noiselessly through the jumble of rock, merging with the shadows and stopping to listen now and then. There were no tell tale sounds to indicate his attacker might also be shifting his position, or none that he heard, and he began patiently working his way, step by step around behind the bushwhacker's last known position. It was slow work, and hot too, but the gunman had played the game many times before and knew his life depended on maintaining absolute silence.

The end, when it came, was shockingly sudden. Johnny's head slowly rose over a boulder and fixed on the petite form of his assailant with surprise. He was only a boy, no more than twelve years old, and small for his age at that, staring fixedly down at the trail as though his target still lay there in plain sight. The gunman pursed his lips and stepped out of cover close behind the lad.

'Drop the gun, boy.'

The youngster's shocked reaction was based on pure fear. He emitted a high-pitched shriek and attempted to slew his gun around to bear on the man who'd surprised him. Johnny, who'd readied himself for just such a reaction, caught the barrel, wrenched it from his grasp and flung it contemptuously aside. One long arm reached out, and a moment later he'd laid hold of the lad too.

'No.' Again the high-pitched squeak, and before the gunman had time to react, the boy had slipped his grip and began to run, darting athletically towards the safety of a rock-strewn slope.

'Oh, no, you don't.' Johnny ground out the threat and flung himself on the kid, who crumpled under his weight. For a moment or two they rolled on the ground, locked together, the slight figure of the fleeing youngster fighting to escape the clutches of the man who pinned him down. All of a sudden he began to sob, and stilled in abject surrender.

'What the hell's going on?' The gunman climbed to his feet and stared at his captive with a look of amazement on his face.

'Don't hurt me. Please don't hurt me.' The words were

desperate, gabbled quickly in a girlish voice.

'Who are you? What's your name?' Johnny already knew he was speaking to the female of the species. She was young and her figure immature, but crushed close beneath him, her burgeoning curves had been clearly apparent.

'Mariella.' She hung her head and spoke in English, but there was a faint trace of an accent in her voice. East European. Most probably her parents were immigrants.

'Why the devil did you shoot at me?' If Johnny Royal had expected the answer to make any sense, he was to be disappointed.

'I thought you were the bogeyman.'

Johnny laughed out loud. The sheer tension following the attack and the slow stalking of his assailant melted away in an instant and he began to laugh uproariously. It took him some time to regain his equilibrium, but when he did he asked the obvious question.

'D'you get many bogeymen around here?'

'No,' the girl replied, looking more confident now her captor had lost his fierce expression, 'but I think they've stolen my pa away.'

'Your pa's been taken by the bogeymen?' Johnny was beginning to feel out of his depth. 'When?'

'A few nights back.' She made an attempt at a shy smile; the man who'd seized her was frighteningly big, but reassuringly friendly considering the circumstances. 'He sometimes goes away on his own, says a man needs to kick over the traces now and then, but this time he was made to leave by the bogeymen and he didn't tell me to mind my manners like he usually does when he goes away.' Her face perked up a little. 'Perhaps he'll come back today.'

'Perhaps,' agreed the gunman. He was no further forward in understanding the situation. 'Where do you live? Is your mother there?'

'Ma left us.' Mariella considered the matter with a serious expression, but no real emotion on her face. 'She left us a long time ago when I was only a baby. Pa's not my real father either, but he's looked after me since my ma left.' She stared at the gunman disconcertingly. 'You're not one of the bogeymen,' she conceded, then went on to elaborate further. 'I live in the cabin down there.' One dirty finger extended down the trail, presumably pointing out the position of a dwelling, though there was none in sight, 'but I don't stay in my room at night any more. That's when the bogeymen come around, so I climb up here to sleep.' Her face crumpled and she began to sob. 'I was late waking and you startled me.' Her tear-laden eyes opened wide in an honest admission. 'I'm sorry if I frightened you, but you were quite safe you know. Pa always told me I couldn't hit a barn door and it looks like he was right.'

Her ingenuous speech didn't reassure the gunman. He wasn't a barn door and at least one of the bullets had come close enough to engender real fear in him. But what could he do with a captive who'd given such compelling reasons for her actions and apologized so sweetly. He gave in and holstered his pistol.

'Have you any other relatives living around here?'

'No.' The girl considered her answer and amended it slightly. 'At least, there is a man who might be a relative, but he only calls on us when it's dark and I haven't seen him since I was little.'

'A man? What sort of man?' Johnny Royal didn't consider his intelligence deficient, but between the bogeymen and a man who might or might not have been a relative, he was beginning to sink into a quagmire that defied rational thought. Answers to that question seemed to elude the girl, too, and she stared uncomfortably at her feet.

'I don't know,' she decided at last. 'I never got to speak to him, but I sometimes used to peek. He always visited late when I was in bed. I don't think he wanted to be seen, especially if there was a posse around. Pa said to tell no one, but I can tell you, can't I?' Mariella opened her eyes wide when she looked up into his face.

'No harm in it,' Johnny smiled back at her, and for a moment the conversation lapsed. 'We'll go to your house,' he made the decision. 'Perhaps your pa's finally taken a notion to returning home.'

'Maybe,' the girl conceded, though it didn't sound as though she really believed any such thing. Then she cast off her gloom and held out her hand, smiling ingenuously. 'I'm glad I didn't shoot you after all.'

'So am I,' replied Johnny with fervent agreement. And let's hope your pa's waiting to take down your britches and tan your hide, he decided privately, though he was careful to keep such satisfying thoughts of sweet revenge to himself.

# CHAPTER TWO

## MOVING IN

'You'd better collect your horse before we go down to the ranch house, mister,' the girl spoke out, obviously willing, even eager, to lead him there. 'There's rustlers around here, as well as bogeymen.' She thought a moment, wrinkling her brow. 'They don't bother Pa much though.' Then she added ingenuously, 'Perhaps that's because we ain't got a lot of stock for them to rustle.'

Johnny Royal felt the predicament. Mariella looked to be resigned to showing him where she lived, but there was no telling whether she'd just light out if he took his eyes off her. On the other hand, though he did wonder if the rustlers were as much in her imagination as the bogeymen, securing his horse was of primary importance. He temporized and picked up the rifle. No sense in leaving temptation in the child's path. 'You can come with me,' he decided.

'My pa once had a horse that came to order whenever he called to it,' she stated blithely while they clambered down the slopes towards the trail. 'He had a special whistle and it always worked.'

'I don't.' Johnny made a flat denial while he stared up the trail to where the animal was grazing in plain sight, several hundred yards up the rise. Damn it to hell, why couldn't the dumb animal have bolted downhill? The sun was sweltering high in the sky and the exposed pass, fed off the blistering heat of the baking rock that hemmed it in, was beginning to feel like a baker's oven. Too hot for chasing horses, that much was certain.

'Perhaps you could train it to come when you call it, too.' She emitted a shrill whistle, presumably an imitation of that used by her father, but it seemed more likely to scare the beast off than entice the animal into scurrying down to them.

Sassy little brat, decided the gunman shortly, biting back on the pithy expletive he almost blasted her with. 'Stop that noise and follow me,' he told her and set off to recover his mount, resigned to the long haul up the trail in the heat of the day. Pray God the horse wasn't too spooked to be caught.

In the event it wasn't, and he was soon leading the docile animal towards Mariella's house. She'd been prattling on all the way down through the pass, but saying nothing to any purpose and the gunman had largely ignored her.

The valley opened up only a few hundred yards down the trail from where he'd been ambushed and the girl immediately cut off into the brush. A small homestead, lingering under a brooding air of neglect, stood close by, just far enough from the trail to be invisible to chance passers-by.

'This is it?'

'Yes,' she told him proudly. 'That's the house, and way by on the left is the new barn.'

Johnny Royal was glad she'd identified which was house, and which barn. Both were in such a poor state of repair he'd have difficulty in telling otherwise. Did she say new barn? It was close on falling down. He ran an experienced eye over the two buildings and their surroundings, clearly the hub of a small ranch. Two corrals: one too run-down for any usefulness; the other in barely better shape, but holding a miserable-looking, rake-thin animal.

'That's Pa's horse,' the girl informed him.

'He's back then.' Johnny's face brightened.

'No,' she replied. 'He didn't ride out.' Her voice took on a hint of the schoolmistress addressing a particularly stupid boy. 'I already told you the bogeymen took him.'

'Did you see them?'

'No. They don't come around until late, and I'm always in bed.' She considered the matter with her head on one side. 'I tried to peep through a hole in the boards once, but Pa saw me looking. He told me they'd take me away and do bad things to me if they saw me watching them.' An admission. 'I didn't try after that, just stuck my head under the blanket.'

'Did he ever see them?'

'Oh yes, he often went out when they came around. To track them, I suppose. Pa's a good tracker.'

'Wasn't he afraid of them, too?'

'Sometimes.' It was a poor answer, but Johnny could see it was the best he was likely to get. In any case if the man's horse was still in the corral, it wasn't likely he'd gone far. He'd already discounted the bogeymen; Mariella's pa clearly knew whoever it was, even went out to greet them. Outlaws perhaps, the way he'd tried to scare the girl from watching them.

He tried a different tack; by the girl's own admission, this wasn't the first time the man had sloped off leaving her on her own. 'Where does your pa usually go to when he leaves you?'

'Down to Miz Morrison's place. She's lives in a big house out of town with lots of bedrooms and lots of women dressed in their under-things. They're real pretty girls, too. I expect that's why Pa goes there such a lot, or maybe it's because she sells hard liquor.'

'How do you know?'

'Everyone knows that!' Having silenced him with a speaking glance, she carried on to explain her personal involvement. 'I went down to her house to collect Pa one time when Sarah wanted him. He wasn't very pleased to see me though. Told me I wasn't ever to go there again.' She looked puzzled. 'I don't know why he said that; he often tells me I'll end up there myself if I'm not careful. Anyhow, he sent me packing, and when he came home he hauled me over to the woodshed and laid into me with his belt.'

'Does he do that a lot?'

'He can't any more; the old woodshed fell down last year.'

Johnny nodded. 'Who's Sarah?' Quite frankly he didn't expect to get a straight answer out of the girl. Nobody who lived around this valley seemed to be quite what they should.

'She lives in the big house a mile or two down the draw. Pa works for her when he's sober.' Mariella bit her lip

19

while she considered the matter. 'Well, she's the one who pays him, but really he works for her grandad who owns all the land hereabouts. He's sick abed and Pa says he's like to die, so Sarah's looking after all the ranch work now. He was a holy terror before he got the shakes.' The girl grinned engagingly. 'Pa says so anyhow.'

Johnny wondered just how old Sarah was. It was a pound to a penny she was barely older than his present charge. 'Is she your friend?'

'Sarah's everyone's friend.' Mariella for once made a positive statement and Johnny guessed it was because she liked the girl. 'She's very pretty, but awful old. Pa says she should have been married off years ago.' The girl made a careful consideration of her companion and added a disconcerting rider. 'She's not as old as you.'

By this time they'd reached the rickety old porch in front of the house. Johnny stepped forward and gingerly prised the door open. It was hung on leather hinges, worn down so far he doubted they'd hold the heavy wood much longer. The inside was dark and cool, as much neglected as the exterior. Dirty, too. It felt empty, but the gunman nonetheless slipped the pistol out of its holster and began to search its murky depths.

There were two rooms only. The filthy living-room, still decorated with the remains of an ancient meal on a rickety wooden table, opened directly off the porch, while behind was a small bedroom complete with wooden pallet. The only other living space was a small platform built under the roof timber and swathed in curtains, which Mariella lost no time in telling him was her own quarters. It was approached by some pegs driven into the dividing wall, and the gunman warily checked it out; no more room than was required to hold a lumpy straw mattress over-thrown by a couple of threadbare blankets.

'Your pa can't have gone far.' Johnny Royal spoke reas-suringly to the girl who was solemnly watching him. 'I might drift on down to Miz Morrison's place and ask after him. He shouldn't have left you alone.'

'I don't mind being alone,' Mariella assured him, 'except when the bogeymen come.' She stared at him, her big eyes pleading. 'Will you stay with me until he returns? You're not scared of the bogeymen.' In truth the gunman's calm confidence, and the way he'd carefully searched the place before holstering his pistol had impressed the girl enough to consider him a potential protector.

Johnny stared at her for a moment before uttering a brief word of assent. Her air of melting innocence was enough to touch any heart less hard than his own, but he casually shrugged off any sense of virtue. He was due a rest, he'd been travelling continuously over the last few weeks. Besides, he still needed time to consider his own father's invitation.

'Thank you.' To the gunman's embarrassment Mariella flung her arms around him and hugged him.

'No more of that,' he decided, quickly shaking her off, 'and I won't stay unless this place is cleaned up.' He rolled up his eyes and made the decision. 'I'll clear the living-room while you make a start on the bedroom.' He stared at her hard. 'I want it spotless. If I'm to stay here, even for a day or two, I expect to live neat and tidy. Where's the broom?'

It was two days before Sarah arrived to roust out her miss-ing ranch hand.

'Good morning, ma'am.' Johnny Royal had heard her arrive, but prudently kept under cover of the barn to which he was making a few urgently needed running repairs, until he could verify the caller's identity. If Mariella was scared enough of the bogeymen to take pot-shots at passing strangers, it stood to reason he also should be wary of their motives, at least until he'd had an opportunity to study them close up. A lone woman on a pony was a different matter. He lounged out of the building and stared at her. A lady, he decided, despite being dressed in work-worn dungarees and a floppy hat that shaded her face.

'Why, hello.' Her voice was open, and she sounded sincerely pleased to see him. A sinuous wriggle and she was out of the saddle and striding across to greet him, pushing her hat back on her head while she walked.

She was tall for a woman, long-legged and lithe, athletic enough to leap off a horse and elegant too, despite her choice of cowboy clothing. Not so old as Mariella had described either, in her middle twenties he'd guess, if that. Not merely pretty either, as he quickly realized, but a beautiful woman. Her even countenance, framed by a mop of tousled straw-blonde hair and clear blue eyes, were as open as her voice, and even the shapeless dungarees couldn't quite disguise the trim curves nestling under the thick material. The hand she held out to take his own in greeting was delicate with particularly long and elegant fingers.

'Sarah McKenzie,' she announced with the merest trace of a Scottish ancestry in her voice. She, too, had used the time it took to walk across the yard to measure the man. A full head taller than herself she'd noted with surprise, and with a broadness of shoulder that indicated unusual strength. A smiling face, dusky with honest work; she'd seen the results of his labour when she'd ridden in. The corrals had been mended; the veranda had been repaired; and if she were any judge he'd been hard at work in the barn. She raised her eyebrows when he held on to her hand longer than strictly necessary, though she didn't attempt to regain it. 'And who are you?'

'Johnny Royal.' He felt a moment's hesitation. The name wasn't well known in this territory, but you never knew where people had travelled, and he didn't want her smile to melt away when she realized he was only a hired gun. As it was, he needn't have worried. She evidently hadn't heard of him.

'Welcome to our valley, Johnny. It's always nice to see someone new. Where's Pieter Rorovitz? Is he around?'

'If you were to ask Mariella she'd tell you the bogeymen took him, but I suspect the wiles of Miz Morrison or one of her girls.' Johnny decided Sarah must be talking of Mariella's pa.

'You've been there?' Sarah thought to take her hand out of his own.

'No. The child told me about the place. I assumed it might be a regular haunt of his. Other than that, I have no more knowledge of his movements than you yourself.'

'I should have realized Pieter wasn't here – he's too lazy even to consider the repairs you've carried out. You must have been here a week.'

'Day before yesterday,' the gunman corroborated casually. 'Not much else to do than furbish the place up a bit. Be more comfortable for the child that way.'

'I don't understand it, Pieter's been gone for at least

ten days.' She frowned, but other than the slightly irrelevant interest he took in the way her nose wrinkled up so cutely, Johnny hardly noticed. 'At least that's the last time he turned up for work at the ranch. Didn't he call you in to look after Mariella?'

'No, ma'am. I met her on the trail. Once I understood she was alone, I offered to stay and look after her until her pa returned. Reckon I ought to go down and see this here Miz Morrison, or I'll be staying forever.'

'No need. Barney set out to find him last night without success. He would have tried her house and any other of his haunts in town.' She smiled again. 'Barney's acting as my foreman for the time being. He's been with us ever since I remember but there's few enough hands left for him to boss.' She took a look around her. 'Where is Mariella? She usually comes out to greet me.'

'Yes, ma'am, you're a particular favourite of hers. Even when you made a mistake as serious as suggesting she was sent to school it didn't lower you in her estimation, though it might have done if her pa had agreed. She's gone into town on the pony today however. I sent her in to collect some supplies – they're sadly depleted and I could hardly expect to live off another man's provisions anyway.'

Sarah stared at the big man. 'She's taken to you, too, by the sounds of things. She doesn't usually talk much to strangers.'

'Reckon she owed me something the way I met her,' grinned the gunman, 'but I lost a lot of my credit when I insisted on cleaning the place up. Got her to take a bath, too; it seems she doesn't think it's natural to wash every day!'

'It was Pieter's mistake to keep Mariella locked away on

her own out here. She's learning all the wrong lessons from him, and she's a bright young thing who could go far with a bit of schooling.'

'What about his wife? What happened to her?'

'I don't know if Elena ever became his wife. She stayed here with him a year or two, then left the two of them flat. Ran off with a gambling man I heard, though I was too young to be told all the details. I dare say she had a lot to contend with; Pieter's never been a provider, but to leave her own child is the outside of enough!'

'Would Pieter do the same?'

'I don't think so, not voluntarily anyway. For all his faults he loves that girl, even if she isn't his own flesh and blood.'

'Where could the man have disappeared to?'

'Into some flesh-pot or other,' Sarah replied angrily. 'He's done it before. Miz Morrison may run the best whorehouse in the valley, but there's other saloons in town, and I dare say Barney may not have tried them all.' She blushed suddenly and excused herself. 'I shouldn't be so blunt, especially in front of a stranger. Grandad would be mortified if he heard I discussed such matters with any man, let alone one I've barely met.' Her face contorted in a fresh outburst of exasperation. 'Damn Pieter's habit of disappearing for days on end. Quite apart from Mariella's situation, I have enough to contend with at the ranch without going on a wild goose chase to find an unreliable hand.'

'If you need someone urgently, I can take Pieter's place until he returns. Fact is, I would have been looking for a job locally anyway. My pockets are about to let right now.' This wasn't strictly true; Johnny Royal might not have been flush, but he had ample for his needs on the trail. His real reason lay in the clear blue eyes of his companion, a prospect attractive enough to put all thoughts of moving on out of his mind for the time being. She pursed her mouth at the offer and Johnny fought down the temptation to kiss it.

'The ranch is that way.' Sarah took the decision without the careful thought she usually applied in taking on a new hand. 'Come and see me tomorrow.' She'd have liked to stay and talk further with the easy going stranger, but that would have been trespassing too far on a first encounter.

# CHAPTER THREE

# BARNEY TOLITTLE

When Johnny Royal arrived at the McKenzie spread bright and early the next morning he was met by the bristling figure of the grizzled old man who was ramrodding the ranch for Sarah. That the foreman wasn't over pleased with his employer's choice of a stranger as a new hand for the ranch, made moreover without consulting him, was soon made evident.

'Damned if I know what young Sarah's about,' the old man began when the gunman swung easily off his horse. 'How in tarnation does she expect me to run this ranch when all she does is pick up riff-raff and stray dogs.' He eyed the gun tied low on his new cowman's right hip with suspicion. 'Darn it,' he cried out with fresh exasperation in his tone. 'I knew she ought never sign on some chance met ne'er-do-well. Are you a gunhand too?'

'Just a drifting cowboy.' Johnny held back his chagrin at the other's annoyance and made a tactful answer while he held out his hand. 'Johnny Royal,' he offered. In truth he

27

was as miffed as the foreman sounded. He'd half expected to see Sarah again, preferably alone, so they could talk, maybe even flirt a little, and now he was saddled with an ageing and distinctly ill-tempered ramrod. Damn it, he wouldn't have come if he'd realized how things were going to be.

'Just you see it stays that way.' The old man was mollified enough to shake hands, though he kept a fierce expression on his face. 'Name's Tolittle, but most everyone calls me Barney. Don't see why you shouldn't.' The foreman's gruff voice had softened at the other's quiet acquiescence of his outburst, but he'd by no means been completely reconciled to the younger man's presence. 'Where'd you work afore? Herding cattle, I mean!'

Johnny tactfully mentioned a few places where he'd done just that, only to find himself on the end of another verbal assault.

'Damned if I see why a man feels the need to drift around so much. Seems some folk can't settle at a job no matter how hard they try. Lazy bunch of wasters if you ask me, just like most of the hands we take on nowadays. Weren't like that when I was young.'

'Did you always work here then?' Johnny felt on much safer ground. Perhaps he could find out more about Sarah. Maybe even solve the mystery of Pieter's disappearance and Mariella's bogeymen.

'No I didn't; damn your eyes for an insolent young hound. I came west with the colonel; Mr Campbell McKenzie as he prefers these days. That was years ago when we were both younger than we are now, but I ain't drifted since, nor intend to do so. Not like the cowardly devils we used to call ranch hands.'

'No offence meant. Sarah told me you'd been a loyal friend of the family a long time. I naturally assumed you'd always worked here.'

'She's Miss McKenzie to the likes of you, and I'll thank you to keep a civil tongue in your head while she's about,' the foreman told him bluntly before admitting the truth in Sarah's assertions. 'Aye, she told you right. I've supported the McKenzies through thick and thin, war and peace, father, son and granddaughter, though I'm damned if I'll lift a finger to aid his worthless grandson.' He went on to explain. 'The old man drove a herd out west after the Confederancy went down and built up this ranch from scratch, carved it out of the barren prairie, fought Indians and rustlers alike. And I was at his side through it all, like I'll continue, unless some bush whacking swine drills me.'

'There's trouble then? Sa—' Johnny caught himself in time and amended his words. 'Miss McKenzie said enough to suggest there might be.'

'Rustlers!' Barney snorted contemptuously. 'Pack of villains the lot of them. Used to leave us alone. Guess we were too strong for them, but since the colonel took to his bed they've grown bolder. Settled on taking cows at first, but recently they've begun bushwhacking the men.'

'That's a dirty business. What's the law doing about it?'

'The sheriff's as lazy a scoundrel as any I've known. He says it's out of town boundaries and he's got no authority. Suggests we call in a federal marshal, even though the nearest is three days' ride and won't take any interest in our affairs without the sheriff referring the evidence to him.'

'How many men have you lost?'

'Two dead, they say, though we never found the bodies. A couple more wounded.' He glared at the new hand. 'No proof in law, you'll say, but they have been intimidating the hands. One man got cut down with a gun in town – self-defence the sheriff reckons, but he was only a boy and barely knew how to shoot. Others have been badly beaten.' The old man threw up his hands in black despair. 'What with the threats and intimidation it soon started a stampede to move on. We had the biggest crew in the valley once upon a time, but now there's hardly a man left, and none of them would ride out alone. Colonel McKenzie's near on dying too; God alone knows what will become of Sarah then, and her cousin's no help to anyone.'

'Her cousin? Is he here?' This was news the gunman hadn't heard before.

'James McKenzie, named after his wastrel of a father; God save me for talking ill of the dead. Damned young whippersnapper arrived here a few weeks ago with a friend in tow. Randy Nolan. Meanest little viper I ever did see. Ties his gun down just like you do. Sight too familiar with Sarah too.' The foreman might be old, but he was still in full possession of all his faculties and he'd seen the way Johnny stiffened, slight though the movement was. 'She don't need no attention from a drifter like you either.' His voice had changed in its pitch and the gunman realized the old man was truly attached to the girl he'd known from birth. 'Don't you go playing with her affections, or you'll have me to deal with.'

Johnny was about to refute the suggestion hotly when he realized that was exactly what he'd planned. A light flirtation, unless the magic of the moonlight took it further.

His lips curled in an humourless smile of self-deprecation; he wouldn't stay around long afterwards, not in a back-woods place like this, nor even at his own family's ranch. Damn the foreman for exposing his weakness.

'Mr Royal.' Sarah's voice was a breath of spring and he immediately forgot his hastily formed intention to move on before he'd ruined yet another life. 'I see you've met Barney already.' She turned to her foreman with genuine affection. 'How's he shaping up?'

'Johnny, ma'am, call me Johnny.' The gunman got his ha'porth in before the old man could reply, although the crusty foreman still managed to surprise him.

'He'll do.' Though he added a rider to depress any pretensions the younger man might hold, 'when there ain't no better around to hire.'

'High praise from you, Barney,' laughed the girl merrily and held out her hand to Johnny. 'You're hired.'

'Thank you, Miss McKenzie.' Johnny took the proffered hand and held on to it longer than he strictly should have.

'Is that your doing, you old fraud?' Sarah turned to accuse her foreman, but made no effort to retrieve her hand for the moment. 'You must call me Sarah,' she smiled up at the gunman, 'not Miss McKenzie. Not ever. Ugh, it makes me sound like an old maid.' She squeezed his fingers gently before disengaging her hand. 'Now be off with the pair of you and earn your pay.'

Ten minutes later the two men were riding out on the prairie.

'I'll give you the tour, and we can cut a few cows out too,' the foreman declared. 'I hear you stayed on here to look after little Mariella?'

'I needed a rest from the trail,' declared Johnny. 'Any case, I'm not travelling anywhere special.' In his present mood of self-recrimination he wasn't willing to be thought of as the girl's benefactor, or to consider continuing on his own journey. 'She's a taking little thing too. Should never have been left alone.'

The old foreman agreed with a grunt. 'Pieter's left her before, but only for a day or two at most,' he told the gunman with the worry clearly audible in the tone of his voice. 'He's been gone eleven days now. Not been seen in town either, nor at Miz Morrison's. Sheriff keeps a keen eye on the saloons in town,' he explained, 'but Miz Morrison's set up her premises over the boundary. Best liquor to be got in a week's ride.' He grinned at his new companion. 'Prettiest set of girls in the territory too.'

'Any other ideas where he could be?'

'No.' Barney Tolittle didn't want to voice his suspicions, not to a virtual stranger. 'What's the girl doing while you're out here all day?'

'I left her some chores,' Johnny replied with a grin. 'Told her to get them done before she ran wild or I'd rebuild the woodshed and instruct her father to take her out there as soon as he reappeared.'

'How'd you meet her?'

Johnny told the story of his ambush to the bemused foreman and asked for some clarification on the matter of bogeymen.

'Damned if I know what to think,' commented Barney. 'Seems to me Pieter didn't want her to know who they were. Mariella may reckon he's a tracker, but I ain't never heard of it. If he went out when they came calling it was to talk to them, which means he knew who they were.' He stroked his beard thoughtfully. 'I sometimes suspected him of trafficking with the rustlers, not that it ever seemed to do him much good. Never had much stock of his own, let alone someone else's.' He grunted in sudden rememberance. 'Young James and that friend of his go out at night too. Can't think they'd have anything to do with Pieter though. They never appeared to recognize him up on the ranch.'

'Never mind. If the bogeymen turn up while I'm still living there, I'll get an answer from them.'

They spent the rest of the day together, riding around the boundaries of the ranch, Barney pointing out landmarks while they continued to talk. The gunman would be sent off to complete some simple task occasionally while the old foreman watched shrewdly on, his initial scepticism grudgingly turning to respect for his new charge's ability.

Late afternoon they saw the smoke.

'Smudge fire.' Barney shielded his eyes from the sun and focused on the wispy cloud that betrayed an unseen fire.

'On McKenzie territory?'

'Reckon so.' Barney wasn't mincing his words. 'Up to no good too.' He turned to the gunman. 'Can you use that gun?'

'I can,' Johnny Royal confirmed, 'but only when it's necessary. We'd better check that smoke out properly before we form any conclusions.'

'The murdering devils have been busy recently. Lost a lot of cattle up this end of the valley.'

'It'd be an unusual rustler who re-branded his ill-gotten gains so blatantly. Any sane man out to run off the stock would do just that; the brand can be changed at leisure once they were safely disposed.'

'How come you know so much about it? You done much rustling yourself?' Barney was watching the gunman suspiciously even while he turned his horse towards the smoke.

'Not rustling precisely.' Johnny suddenly realized that to an honest man it would have been just that. 'I was caught up in a range war,' he temporized with a brief explanation. 'We ran some beef off in revenge,' and cursed his own guilt while he spurred his mount in Barney's wake.

'Four of the devils; and we've got them dead to rights.' Barney mouthed the words softly to his companion on the ridge that fringed a shallow depression with a brackish lake at its centre and a patch of woodland on the far side. They'd dismounted half a mile back, taken out their rifles and made their approach in silence. 'Cattle gather here in the heat of the day, plenty of good water for them,' he explained.

In fact there were no loose cattle in sight, but thirty or forty head were gathered in a rough corral, made by collecting up the loose brush that lay around in plenty. Two of the men were mounted and patrolling the limits of this makeshift corral, while the other pair were gathered around a small fire examining the implements in its depths. Johnny, just like any other cowboy, knew a branding iron when he saw it.

'Hold on, old-timer,' he advised when Barney showed a marked preference to face the men down immediately. 'Don't go off half cocked. Those men are acting a damned sight too casual for wrongdoing. Either those cattle aren't

McKenzie's, or they've set a guard.'

'They're McKenzie cows all right, I'd wager my life on it,' declared the foreman belligerently. His bright eyes began to scan to ridge. 'Those arrogant bastards believe they can get away with daylight robbery,' he carried on. 'There's no guard set or we'd never have managed to creep up on them. The country around here's too open for a sentry to miss us.'

'True.' Johnny Royal continued to watch for signs the rustlers had set a watch. Not that the old man wasn't right; they would have been spotted for sure unless the damned fool was asleep. He shrugged. 'Reckon they felt safe out here; didn't you tell me the other hands won't budge less'n they have a partner?'

Barney Tolittle didn't bother to answer, just stood up and began to stride angrily down the slope towards the men in the depression. They, in turn, stopped work to watch his progress with unfeigned interest. Shrugging his shoulders with fatalistic determination, the gunman trailed in the wake of the old man, still searching the hillside around him. He caught the flash of sunlight on the barrel a moment before it was fired.

'Look out! Get down, Barney,' he cried and sprang forward post haste to throw the old man down into the dubious cover of some acacia. It wouldn't stop bullets, but it hid their movements from their enemies until they could make it as far as more substantial shelter. 'For God's sake keep moving, they'll have our position marked.' The gunman slithered snake-like through the thickest of the vegetation, ignoring the thorns that sliced into his skin and drew the old-timer behind him. 'You all right?' he asked.

'One of them murdering varmints winged me.' The foreman hissed in pain when he rolled deeper into the bushes.

Johnny at last realized Barney was hit, but he couldn't take time out to investigate how badly until he knew the dispositions of their enemies. Without that knowledge they would both be in danger of losing their lives and until then the foreman would have to look after himself. He strung together what he already knew. All four of the rustlers who'd been in the depression had disappeared, those mounted probably under cover of the trees, the others in some sort of prepared position. Their approach must have been noted and the opportunity taken to prepare an ambush using the four as bait. A further burst of fire off the hillside rattled through the undergrowth well wide of them and he grunted in satisfaction before turning his attention on his wounded companion.

'Is it bad?'

'It's not fatal, but it's damned painful.' Barney's voice was stretched thin by the pain of his wound which worried the gunman more than his anger ever had.

Twisting athletically, Johnny conducted a brief examination of his companion's wound. 'Caught a slug in your upper arm,' he informed the old foreman succinctly. 'It may have broken the bone, or chipped it at least. No sign of an exit wound either.' Thank God there's no great amount of bleeding he could have added while he loosened his kerchief and began to roughly bind the wound up. 'This'll have to do for the present,' he decided. 'You're lucky not to be worse hit, there're at least two men up on the slopes.'

With those final words he slithered away under cover of

the tough acacia bushes, mentally cursing the thorns that ripped at his stout clothing. He knew they were dead men unless they could make better cover, and even then the odds were against them. These were no ordinary rustlers; these men were killers who could murder in cold blood from ambush. Barney's rifle spat fire somewhere behind him and he thanked God for the tough old man's spirit. He'd draw their fire with a display like that, and their attention too. Let me get up on the hill, he prayed, and I'll have a go at evening up the odds.

So it proved. Cover of the acacia bush ran out ten yards short of a shallow cliff and Johnny was forced to make a run at it, but with a spirited battle still going on behind him, he made it unseen. This was no time for hesitation; Barney's cover was flimsy in the extreme, and although he had no doubt the old man would change position every time he fired, it was only a matter of time before another bullet found him. The gunman took the slope at a run and dived into the rocks at its summit. He swung his rifle around and fired. His first target was down by the lake where the men had dug some sort of trench to take cover in, but it wasn't deep enough to shelter them from this angle and they cut and ran when they realized they were in his sights.

He aimed deliberately at one running man only to see his shot go wide when his aim was spoiled by the whang of a ricocheting slug that howled off the rock a few inches from his head. He flung himself deeper under cover and turned his rifle on his new attackers, but the rustlers were retreating and by the time he'd set himself the two mounted rustlers had led horses forward for their companions and begun to light out. Further hoof-beats behind him indicated the two remaining on the hill were also retreating. He fired a single snap shot to send them on their way and he trailed down the hillside to where Barney waited.

'He'll be all right,' Sarah informed Johnny a few hours later. Barney had been laid to bed in the ranch house following an emergency operation by one of the ranch's Chinese wranglers who knew enough about doctoring to take the lead. He'd deftly removed the slug together with some splinters of bone, but dismissed any idea the bone might be broken.

'Is sore,' he admitted in shattered English, 'but no bone broken. I know, I tend horse many time.'

'What happened?' Sarah wanted a report from the gunman as soon as the Chinaman had left.

'We caught out some rustlers red-handed and went in to question them. Unfortunately they'd already spotted our arrival and were laying for us. Once they'd drawn us in, they opened up and caught us in a cross fire. Barney was hit, but still game, and the rustlers ran off once they realized there were no easy pickings.' Johnny Royal kept his explanation strictly to the facts.

'Barney was lucky he had you with him,' the girl stated simply. 'He knows he'd be dead by now, if you'd cut and run.' Sarah's eyes dropped and she made a startling confession. 'I'm glad you're here too.' The heat ran into her face and she changed the subject abruptly, realizing she was in danger of saying too much to someone who was still a virtual stranger. 'With all this shooting going on I think you should bring Mariella to work with you tomorrow. I don't like to think of her left alone. You can both dine here too.'

'Thanks, it'll take an invitation like that to save me from her wrath. It's been dark for a couple of hours now, and I promised her I'd be back home in daylight.'

# CHAPTER FOUR

# VISITORS

The old ranch house was quiet as the grave. Johnny Royal slid off his horse and approached it warily. If rustlers were Mariella's bogeymen, he'd seen enough that day to realize they were prepared to shoot first and ask questions later. Was that what had happened to Pieter? If so, where was the body?

And where the devil was Mariella? A swift search of the environs revealed no sign of rustlers or bogeymen and Johnny strode into the house, where the rooms were as dark as the surrounding night. He struck a match and lit a couple of candles in their sconces.

'Mariella,' he called fearfully, knowing a moment of apprehension that she too might have been attacked and kidnapped, or even killed.

The girl didn't answer, but a whimper of fear led him to her bed in the rafters. The slightest of rustles gave her away. She'd burrowed down into the straw that made up her mattress until she was completely hidden. The state of her nerves was revealed when his hand investigated the makeshift shelter and she leapt out with a shriek. A moment later she was in his arms shuddering and crying, moaning over and over again. 'You're back. You're back.'

'What happened?' Even with the doubtful light thrown by the evil-smelling tapers it had taken only a momentary glance to reveal that nothing of importance was missing or out of place. From there it was only a small step to deduce there'd been no intruders.

'The bogeymen. They came.'

'Came where?'

'Outside. I heard them; they were standing over by the old cottonwood. I could see their shadows, and they were breathing fire and smoke.'

Johnny disengaged himself from the girl's embrace and scooted down into the room below to peer out of the window. 'They've gone,' he breathed, more to calm down the girl than in any belief, either of their leaving, or of their coming in the first place. 'Wait here.'

On that final command the gunman slipped out the house and cautiously flitted through the undergrowth, approaching the old cottonwood by a circuitous route. It was dark, but his questing fingers quickly located the stub of a cigar. Mariella had been right; someone had concealed themselves in the shadows under the old tree to watch the house. Were they waiting for Pieter? Or was it he himself who was now their focus?

'They've gone.' He kept his observations short in front of Mariella, not wanting to frighten her any more than she already was.

'They ran away when you came,' she told him in return. 'Don't go away again tomorrow.' Then suddenly burst into a flood of girlish tears that unnerved him more than the knowledge that someone had the house under surveillance. 'I thought you'd gone and left me like Pa. You won't, will you?' she pleaded.

'I'll take you with me tomorrow,' he assured her awkwardly, not at all used to the unfamiliar role of protector. 'Sarah's asked us both to supper. Now get yourself off to bed and forget about the bogeymen.'

Next morning Johnny was out and about early, and first off he checked out the old cottonwood again. No less than three cigar butts lay in its shadow along with a lone stogie. He frowned in concentration. At least two men were watching the house, though the reason for their vigil still wasn't clear.

Were they waiting for Pieter to return? Perhaps, but in a closed community like the valley, news of his reappearance would travel fast. No need to wait out in the dark unless they needed to speak to him urgently. There again, if their business couldn't wait, why hadn't they appeared the previous night also? Three cigars suggested they'd waited for some time too. Why? Urgent business to do with the ranch perhaps, but then they'd left as soon as he arrived, which suggested otherwise.

Mariella? Unlikely since she'd been alone in the house and vulnerable. If they'd wanted the child, they could have taken her easily. The mere thought sent a shiver down his spine and he mentally castigated himself for not taking the girl's bogeymen stories seriously enough. The house too could be crossed off the list. Mariella had slept rough and left it empty on several occasions since Pieter left.

Were they watching for him then? Any logic in the

reasoning behind that was even less clear. He'd only just arrived on the scene and whoever the bogeymen were, it was unlikely they could have any real interest in an unknown drifter.

Two men rode in before he made it back to the house where Mariella was busy frying up breakfast on the skillet.

'Howdy.' Johnny kept the welcome short. Something about them told him they were on a mission.

'Mr Royal.' The younger man spoke first.

'Speaking.' Johnny Royal carefully looked him over before dismissing him as a threat. He was a pasty-faced youth with a softness to his willowy body that suggested he'd never set himself to a stroke of honest labour in his life. Handsome enough in a pale kind of way, but with a weak chin and diffident manner that suggested a lack of true backbone. He wore a gun, but there was nothing about the man to suggest he could use it with any facility.

His companion was an entirely different matter. He was as dark as the other was fair, and he regarded the gunman with a hooded stare reminiscent of a coiled snake about to strike at its prey. A ragged scar ran across his right cheek, pulling down the eye on that side and spoiling what might otherwise have been regarded as good, if broodingly dark, even satanic looks. His hand lay close to the gun at his hip and even a cursory glance told Johnny that both the holster and the pistol within were well used. This was a dangerous man.

'James McKenzie.' The younger man spoke again. 'I'm staying up at my grandfather's place.'

Johnny nodded. 'So I heard. I won't ask you to step down, I'm working up there myself and I'll be late if I entertain visitors.'

'That's what I came about.' The young McKenzie's voice trailed off when Johnny Royal's eyes met his own. He dropped his gaze, 'and to ask if Pieter had been found, of course.'

'I haven't seen Pieter.' The gunman faced the man down, wondering what he wanted, glad too he had his pistol handy. If he'd been out chopping wood he'd probably have been caught unarmed, and even though the two of them didn't seem anxious to start hostilities immediately, he still felt safer with a gun at hand.

'Fact is, I wanted to look you over. Poor Sarah has a lot to do on the ranch what with all this rustling going on, and I didn't want her being taken advantage of by any stray drifter.'

'Do I pass muster?' Johnny didn't really care. What the devil did it have to do with Jamie McKenzie? From all he'd heard the old man had cut both father and son out of his inheritance.

'Frankly.' The young man paused. 'Well—'

'What he means to say is no.' The other man broke in decisively. He looked as though he was enjoying his companion's floundering and deliberately took out a cigar and lit it before going on. 'Tell him how it is, Jamie.'

'Well—'

Johnny ignored Jamie McKenzie and turned his attention on the older man, raising his eyebrows in a questioning fashion. 'And you are?'

'Randy Nolan.' The name tugged at the gunman's memory, but recalling the circumstances proved elusive. 'I heard you were getting a mite too friendly with Sarah.' He blow out a cloud of smoke and laid his hand on the well-worn grips of the pistol in its holster.

'What's that to you?' The gunman failed to react to the veiled threat. Nolan might have been a fast draw specialist, but he was sitting awkwardly in the saddle and Johnny was confident enough in his own skill that if it came to gunplay his pistol would be first into the fray.

'Randy's affianced to my cousin,' James broke in. 'Don't want to announce it yet, not with my grandfather so close to death, but the two of them are veritable love-birds.'

Randy Nolan smirked and barked out a short laugh. 'Guess I'll be claiming her in a day or two,' he confirmed. 'The old man's just about cashed in his chips.'

'Not quite how Sarah put it,' the gunman told them mildly. 'Now, if you don't mind, I'll go and eat. There's a lot of work to get through up at the ranch.'

'No need. You're fired.' Randy Nolan provided the words, but Jamie McKenzie nodded weakly to confirm them. 'I'd advise you to leave the valley, too, ain't no one wants a damned vagabond hanging around.'

'I was taken on by Miss Sarah,' Johnny reminded them. 'I'll let her decide whether I stay or not.' He turned away and walked deliberately towards the old ranch house, wondering if he'd done right in turning his back on them. Nolan, at least, would have no hesitation in gunning a man down from behind, and he heaved a sigh of relief when he heard their horses wheel and ride out.

Mariella had hidden herself again, but it didn't take much reassurance to winkle her out of her cot again.

'Were those men your bogeymen?'

'No, but they're bad men,' she told him, earnestly regarding his face for signs that he believed her.

'I thought they might have been.' He didn't tell the girl

45

about the cigar butts. 'You told me you'd seen the bogey-men when they took your pa?'

'Yes. I peeped out when they were talking to him.'

'Just the two of them?' Johnny still wondered if his visitors and the bogeyman were one and the same.

'No. There was a whole gang of them, and they were threatening him.'

'How do you know?'

'He was frightened.' A cloud passed across the girl's face and Johnny stopped the inquisition. Poor girl, she was scared stiff too.

The days passed quickly after that. Mariella accompanied Johnny to the ranch where she was left in the charge of the cook, an amply endowed woman who'd once been Sarah's nurse, while he got on with work on the ranch. To Johnny's surprise, and in the absence of any other hand, Sarah herself usually donned thick, mannish work gear to help out, proving as good in the saddle as either he or Barney.

Every evening, too, they dined at Sarah's table, with Barney joining them to act as duenna. If he ever thought that Sarah and Johnny were getting too intimate, he was wise enough not to say anything to either of them. Johnny knew it though, a surprisingly warm feeling. He'd had a lot of women over the years, not all of them painted harpies either, but none like this. He wanted to be with her, not just to tumble her, but to live with her. Damn it, he castigated himself in a moment of lucidity, what the devil would a lady want with a wastrel like Johnny Royal? And Sarah was a lady! He knew it, just as she did, though they might both choose to forget it if the situation was right.

He hadn't seen James or his crony again and asked Sarah about this one evening. Mariella had fallen asleep and been put to bed at the ranch, while Sarah walked out to the stable with Johnny where his horse waited for him.

'Is your cousin still around?' he asked in a puzzled voice. 'We never see them about. Not even at dinner.'

'They're still here,' confirmed his companion while they leaned on the rails of a corral. 'They lie abed until we've all been working the range for hours, then they stay out late every night. Much too late. They never say where, but I'd lay my money on Miz Morrison's.'

'What are they doing here? They don't seem the type to hanker after a ranch, and I gather your grandfather is no friend to the boy.'

'I've no idea why they stay here, nor even why they came. Jamie's never made any attempt to see his grandfather, nor anyone else I know of come to that. I tried to keep their visit a secret to avoid sending Grandad into a rage, but I think he knows they're here, though he never speaks of it. I'd throw them out but for the trouble they'd cause. I'm not afraid for myself, but I can't have Grandad put into a pelter in his condition.'

'They give you any trouble?' Johnny couldn't help moving his right hand to hover menacingly over the well-oiled leather of his holster. The thought of Nolan making up to Sarah gnawed at his heart.

Sarah caught a glimpse of the instinctive motion and smiled in the gathering dark. 'Don't,' she begged. 'He's a killer.' Her hands clutched at his arm and she leaned in closer. 'He still attempts to act the gallant when he sees me, but neither of them will make a move while Grandad's alive.' She smiled again. 'He's still a formidable old man

47

when he wants to be.'

'Barney told me he was real sick, like to die anytime. If that's true, how long will his reputation continue to protect you?'

'Long enough. He may be weak, but he's not ready to give up yet. He wants to see you too.'

'Me?' Johnny was surprised. 'How the devil does he know about me? I'm only a temporary ranch hand.'

'I told him about you.' Sarah leaned in closer still, trying to tell herself it was only concern for his anxiety that drove her. 'You don't mind, do you?' She tipped back her face to look up at him and swayed unsteadily forward until they were touching.

Johnny felt the heat of her body against his own and the inevitable happened. One arm slipped around her waist to draw her even closer while he dropped a kiss on her cool, soft lips. He drew back, afraid he might have gone too far; she'd never played the coquette with him like so many of the women he'd known.

'I thought you'd never get around to it.' Sarah surprised him by subsiding into his embrace and lifting up her face to be kissed again.

He kissed her deeply this time, holding the embrace for long, entrancing minutes while she snuggled further into his arms. The warmth of her body soaked into his own, the thrust of her breasts stiff against his powerful chest, the weight of her hips arching against the thrust of his own burgeoning desire. She drew back suddenly, her eyes gleaming.

'You'll have something to talk about with Grandad now,' she told him tartly. 'First thing tomorrow. He's always awake early.' Sarah kissed him hard on the lips once more and swung away, breaking their embrace. 'Good night,' she told him coolly and headed for the house.

'Good night.' Johnny's voice was thick with freshly stirred lust and he shivered in helpless reaction. The sudden onset of passion had hit him more powerfully than he'd ever expected, and if he'd known just what wicked, unbidden thoughts were going through Sarah's mind while she walked away he'd have dragged her into the soft baled hay in the stable there and then.

Good night! It sure was, and Johnny left with a smile on his face and elation in his heart.

# CHAPTER FIVE

# THE FLYING T

'Guess there's no need for you to watch over Mariella tonight.' Barney broke into Johnny's thoughts while he was still watching the door through which Sarah had disappeared. 'How's about you and me taking a look-see at Miz Morrison's?'

Johnny regarded the old man carefully. 'You crept up mighty quiet,' he commented, wondering just how much the foreman had seen. Then, not caring any more. 'How's the arm?'

'It's a mite painful sometimes, but I can use it when I have to. Nothing a glass or two of good hard liquor wouldn't cure. How about it?'

'Sure.' Johnny clapped the old-timer on the back. 'I didn't feel like going back to an empty house anyhow.'

The two men confined themselves to idle chit-chat while they walked their mounts down the trail towards town. Johnny hadn't ridden that way himself and was almost disappointed when Barney turned his horse off the main trail a mile or so short of the first houses. Miz Morrison's place wasn't the jerry-built shack he'd expected, more of a mansion in miniature, even down to the garden surrounding its impressive façade and elegant, colonnaded porch.

'Looks expensive,' he commented with a glance at his companion.

'It can be,' agreed Barney, 'but they run the best goddamned bar in these parts, or any other I know. It's the gambling and girls that bring in the money, the bar's just run to get the punters in. Honest tables I'm told, but there's some high rollers hereabouts and many a green-horn's lost his shirt. Girls are prime too.'

'The drink will suit me fine.'

'Me too.' The old foreman looked a bit sheepish when he slid off his horse and tied it loosely to the hitching post, already occupied by a number of other mounts. 'Look,' he continued with the evident intention of getting something off his chest. 'Don't take this the wrong way, but I've known Sarah for a long time. If the colonel was on his feet I wouldn't have to do this, but he's not.' He paused, wondering how to put his feelings into words that wouldn't offend a companion he was beginning to feel real affection for.

Damn, thought Johnny, so the shrewd old buzzard had seen something, or at least had his suspicions raised. 'Go ahead, Barney,' he ordered ruefully. 'Tell me what's on your mind.'

'We'll talk out here,' decided the old foreman. 'Miz Morrison's house isn't a place I'd care to discuss the affairs of a lady like Sarah.'

'True enough. What do you want me to tell you? I don't

know what you saw, but truth is, there isn't a lot to tell.'

'Never you mind what I saw tonight. What I see most every day is that Sarah's mighty partial to you, too particular to be lavished on a man who's just drifting to no purpose. What she needs is a man who's ready to settle down, not one she'll pine for when he's gone.'

'Are you suggesting marriage?' Johnny had expected Barney to warn him off again, not play matchmaker.

'That's between the two of you; ain't none of my business. Not any of it really,' admitted the old man, 'but I love Sarah like she's my own bairn.' He paused as though gauging Johnny's reaction. 'You ain't just a drifting cowboy either; you use that gun like you were born to it. Drifting or running it don't matter, don't play with her affections. Her pa's dead and likely her grandad too in the next few weeks. She'll be all alone in the world after that.'

'She'll have you,' Johnny pointed out. He should have been angry with his companion for interfering, but instead he found himself agreeing with the ornery old varmint. Damn, but he was getting soft. Liking a tough old buzzard so much he'd let the man criticize his lifestyle, and left in transports by a simple kiss from a girl he merely intended to trifle with. Or was that all he wanted? For once the gunman had no slick answer ready, not even for himself.

'Aye,' Barney replied, 'but it's you she wants, poor little fool.' He shook his head sorrowfully. 'Not that you ain't a better choice than that friend of Jamie's, Randy Nolan.'

'I'll not hurt her if I can help it.' Johnny Royal was more surprised by the vehemence in his voice than his companion who just nodded sagely.

'Reckon you won't, son.' With that he turned and

strode towards the door, a strangely satisfied smile on his face.

The wide doorway led directly into a bar that, although more ornate than most, matched many of those Johnny had patronized in the past. Over the years he'd learned to look past the first impression, but nothing seemed out of place and he followed Barney to the polished mahogany bar-top with an admiring whistle on his lips.

'Not quite what I expected from what Mariella told me,' he admitted. His eyes lit on an elegantly dressed young woman engaged in conversation with a couple of early evening customers. If she was typical of the girls employed by the house, the whores were indeed as prime as Barney had suggested, and he admitted as much to his companion.

'We'll take our drinks and sit over there.' Barney pointed to a table in a remote corner of the bar.

Johnny was ready to demur to the suggestion they sit so far out of the way, but the foreman was already walking that way and the gunman could only shrug his shoulders and follow.

'What did Mariella have to say?'

'That all the girls spent their time in their underwear.' Johnny was sure Barney had no interest in what Mariella had told him; indeed no interest in anything other than the noisy bunch of cowpokes sitting around a couple of tables they'd pushed together. He surveyed them surreptitiously too, but unable to see anything strange about them, gave the foreman a warning kick.

'Must have been down here in the morning after her pa.' Barney misunderstood the warning. 'Like as not they'd be in their underwear or even less about then.

Came down to collect Pieter once myself and Miz Morrison invited me in for breakfast. Never saw so much bare flesh in one day in my life, and a froth of white lace to show it off too. Damned fancy under-things they wore.'

'For God's sake, Barney,' Johnny hissed. 'Leave off eyeballing those men before they realize you got some interest in them.'

The old man started, suddenly realizing he was staring too intently. 'Flying T,' he hissed. 'They're too drunk to recognize us, especially when we're holed up in this corner well out of their way, but look at the one on the far left. Reckon we saw the spitting image of him a couple of days back.'

Johnny looked again, concentrating on the man Barney had marked. He nodded. 'You're right,' he confirmed. 'He was one of the rustlers. Stood by the fire in plain sight. Guess he didn't expect us to live long enough to identify him. None of the others looks familiar though.'

'I always did suspect the Flying T. They're a strange outfit; always seem to employ more men than they have cows, rough fellows at that. I guess they keep the cattle out of our sight in case we identify the new-burned brands. Come to that they were always selling. Struck a big beef contract with the army, I heard.'

'Will the sheriff believe us?'

'Maybe, maybe not. He won't act though. We're well out of town limits here.'

'He's still a lawman.'

'He reckons it's federal business.' Barney looked concerned. 'It'd take a week to fetch the marshal, even if he'd come. It's our word against theirs when all's said and done. Not exactly the sort of evidence to tempt a man into a long, hard ride. Even if he is the only law we've got around here.'

'You'd better go before you're recognized,' Johnny advised his companion. 'I'm a stranger to the valley. I can get closer, maybe even eavesdrop. You live here; they may be drunk, but they'll know you for sure.'

Once he'd convinced the foreman to leave, Johnny strolled over to the bar again, ostensibly to buy another drink, but in reality to provide him with an excuse to sit at a table nearer his quarry. Evening was beginning to turn into night and more girls were beginning to sashay into the room as custom grew steadily. The gunman marked out a tall blonde who was surveying the bar from behind the cowboys, and straight way strode over to introduce himself, ushering her to a chair at a table close by the rustlers.

'I'll take champagne,' she told him confidently and sat back to observe him while he called a barman over.

Johnny Royal thought she was weighing up just what she could take him for, and was surprised by her follow-up. 'Just what do you want, fellow? Ain't me, that's for sure.'

'Isn't it?' The gunman recovered himself by lifting her hand to his lips, then settled back, attempting to concentrate on the lady and still hear what the rustlers had to say. 'What's your name?'

'Mary.' She announced her name in flat tones. 'Do you want to drink that champagne in my room?'

Johnny was way too slow with his answer.

'I didn't think so.' She leaned forward. 'I done my bit for the saloon by getting you to order the champagne, but I'm a working girl too. If there's nothing else you want, I'll be going.'

The gunman was uneasily aware she'd raised her voice and several of the nearby Flying T crew were staring at them.

'Your prerogative.' The rustlers hadn't said a word about business. Admittedly, he hadn't been within earshot for long, but the gunman suspected they were in town for a night's entertainment and unlikely to discuss any of their future plans. Nevertheless, while they were here, it might be the perfect opportunity to visit their ranch. He doubted the entire crew were in town, but the group was big enough to convince him most of them must be.

The Flying T land adjoined the McKenzie spread and Johnny Royal found no difficulty in detecting the trail that led to its ranch house, which provided a disappointingly normal face to the outside world. The main house, candlelit in more than one window, perhaps a bit smaller and less grand than the McKenzies', but nevertheless impressive. The barns were more widespread than he might have guessed for a rustler hide-out and he could hear animals moving about in the corrals, though it was too dark to make them out.

He dismounted and prepared to take a closer look on foot. His own native caution had been sharpened by years of living on the edge, so he took nothing for granted. The ranch shouldn't have been guarded, but it was. Stealing through a corral occupied by two complacent-looking cows he marked the first in an entrance to one of the barns. The low glow of a cigarette marked the spot, and forewarned Johnny hunkered down to study the ranch more closely. There was a second close to the main house, sitting down by the main door with a rifle across his lap, betrayed by choosing a seat too close to the flickering light of a nearby window. The rustler boss inhabited the house, he guessed, and the hands would use the bunk house built in its shadows. Big enough to accommodate more men than were drinking at the saloon, he noted with some trepidation.

He slipped forward again, confident the sentries wouldn't see him now he knew where they were. Concentrating on the house, he scurried across the ground in short bursts, slithering through the shadows, then stopping to listen before the next advance. At last he reached the wall around a corner from the guard and candlelit windows, one of which he was sure would give him a lead.

Foiled by the sentry's position from listening under the windows themselves, he began to look around for a convenient point to break into the house. No sooner had he marked a likely window, however, than he heard movement from in front. Giving up on his schemes to mount a break-in, he scooted down the wall to the corner again, peering around in time to hear an incoming group of riders hallooing to the house. The sentry was distracted and he saw his opportunity; a moment later saw him in the shadows of the porch, perfectly placed to see and hear what the men had to say.

Two or three men emerged from the porch to hear the incoming riders report. Johnny couldn't see them from his position, though they were no more than feet away from him, but he formed the impression these were the leading lights of the rustling organization.

'There's someone spying out the land, boss.' The leading rider was the same man that Barney had pointed out in the saloon. He went on to explain. 'We saw him at Miz

Morrison's talking to one of the girls. Didn't take much notice at first, but there was something familiar about him. The boys and I got to talking and decided he looked a lot like the gunman who sided with Barney Tolittle when we sprung our trap on him last week. Come to think of it, Barney was in himself earlier. We cornered the girl and made her talk, not that she knew much. Seemed he used her to get closer to our table.'

'Did he hear anything?' The tone was deep and measured. The rustler boss wasn't a man who panicked easily.

'No, boss, that's the truth. He left real quick once he realized we'd seen him. By the time we'd identified him he was long gone, but Santos reckoned he was heading this way. He tracked him a while, but even Santos couldn't do much in the dark.' Johnny took heed of the name; Santos was evidently a tracker of some note.

'He's here.' The interruption was made in a flat, guttural tone.

'How do you know?' The rustler boss turned his attention on an obvious half-breed, dark as a pure-bred Indian, but dressed entirely as his white companions. 'Where is he?'

'I feel it,' explained the Indian. 'He is close by.' He listened with his head on one side. 'I heard the echo of his horse when we rode in, snickering at the sounds we made.'

'Why didn't you take him?'

'The horse was alone. He is here.'

'Goddamn you, Santos.' The mounted man began to search around, turning his head this way and that without success. 'He can't be here, we got guards posted.'

'Circle your men wide,' commanded his boss, still confident. 'If he has sneaked in, he won't get out. Search out his horse too.'

Like Hell, decided the gunman, confident he could slip past this rabble now he knew their plans. He took a chance on peeking at them; Santos was the one to avoid. He was nothing to look at, but evidently had a talent for tracking, and would be hard to fool.

'Why not leave him to me? I can take him up at the ranch.' Johnny stiffened, recognizing the voice. Randy Nolan! So was this where he came every night? Was Jamie McKenzie in with the rustlers, too?

'Just stick to your own task.' The rustler boss dismissed the suggestion without thinking. 'I need you in residence ready to act when we make our move. If this new hand's half as thick with the boss's daughter as you seem to think, then she won't want you around once you've picked a quarrel with him.'

What the devil did Randy Nolan know about his relations with Sarah? Had he been spying on them? Johnny Royal began to back up, sliding on to his belly when a couple of lanterns were brought into play. He was too far away by this time to hear what was being said, but the group broke up and began to ride in different directions, evidently in an attempt to form a cordon around the house. He grinned and slithered off to his left, mentally congratulating himself on leaving his horse way off. Searching the house could wait; he now knew there was some connection between Nolan and the rustlers, probably Jamie McKenzie too. What were they after? Well, he was no nearer to answering that question, but it wasn't just rustling a few cows. The ranch itself maybe, since they apparently needed an inside man in place when they committed themselves.

He took in a group of riders circling their mounts in his path and cut across a corral full of freshly branded cattle, the smell of burnt hide still overriding their own scent. They regarded him with steady, bovine stares, but didn't stir while he flittered through their midst. He ducked under the rail, a mere dozen yards from the nearest rider and scuttled unseen across the trail and into some brush. Once hidden he moved more slowly, treading carefully so no twig would crack and announce his presence. He was outside the circle barring his way now, and nothing could prevent his escape.

So it seemed. A couple of minutes later he was back in the clearing where he'd left his mount and about to step into the open when his well-honed instincts cut in. There was nothing obviously wrong, just a feeling that his horse was more nervous than it had a right to be. It knew he was near, but that wasn't enough to spook the animal. A predator perhaps?

And then he knew.

He felt the attack before it was properly launched, pure gut feeling jolting him into a frantic dive to his left, leaving his right hand free to collect his pistol. He hit the ground rolling, his gun already half drawn. The half-breed's attempt to take him by surprise had failed, but he was as quick a killer as any the gunman had faced and stuck out one flailing leg as his spring-heeled leap over-shot his intended target. A foot shod in supple leather slammed into Johnny's fist and the pistol slewed wildly across the tiny clearing.

Both men scrambled to their feet on the instant, Johnny desperately backing up to gain time while he snatched his own knife from its scabbard. Though he was a barely visible shadow in the dark, the gunman could sense that the breed had a triumphant smirk on his face when he advanced. Quite right too, Johnny told himself in self-castigation. He'd been out-foxed all the way around. He'd heard the half-breed tell of his horse; he should have been ready for the man to appear there, should have been the one to surprise the breed, not the other way around. Damn it, a day or two around a pair of sparkling eyes and he'd forgotten how quickly a man could die.

Warily he circled left, flexing his right hand to work out the stiffness induced by the numbing kick it had received. For a moment he'd panicked that some bones might have been broken, but evidently not, for feeling was beginning to return, and he gripped the knife more firmly. The breed was stalking him, but still hadn't called his fellow conspirators for aid. He was too confident in his own ability, Johnny decided, probably with good reason, but his attacker, too, could make mistakes. One should never underestimate an opponent.

The shadows seemed to bunch and a sudden silhouette sprang up, stark against a patch of sky. Johnny whirled, throwing up his left arm to defend himself, while his own knife-arm slashed wildly at the proffered target. He felt a stinging pain when his own forearm was sliced open, and, almost simultaneously, the warmth of fresh blood flowing off his own knife. Honours even, he decided. His own wound was no more than a gash in the flesh, while a spectral laugh told him the half-breed was no more incapacitated than himself.

'Prepare to die, white man.'

The guttural uttering came from a totally unsuspected

position behind the gunman, but although the half-breed's chilling ability to manoeuvre unseen and unheard in the dark of the night was unsettling, Johnny had no intention of losing his composure. He shifted his own position, aware the attack wouldn't come from the same direction as the voice.

He was right. It was as though the shadows of the night solidified into human form, but for once the half-breed had an enemy worthy of his skill. Johnny had fought Indians before, and he'd fought in the dark too. He gave way before the weaving knife of his opponent, dropping back into a less sheltered clearing among the trees, then feinted himself before closing with the dark shadow of his enemy. Hand-to-hand they struggled, the Indian unable to break away from the ferocious grip Johnny had fastened on him. He twisted the wrist under his left hand until the bones began to crack, and with a wordless cry of pain the Indian dropped his weapon.

They staggered and the half-breed fell back, dropping to the floor and rolling in a desperate attempt to evade the gunman's hold. Johnny too lost his knife but held fast on to his opponent. The gunman was the bigger by a head and manifestly by far the stronger. At close quarters the fight was his, but he knew if the half-breed slipped loose, it was only a matter of time before the Indian's innate ability to disappear and noiselessly shift position at will would count against him. The next attempt on his life would no doubt be made with a gun!

The half-breed, too, was desperate. He attempted to cry out to his companions, unseen but no doubt still within earshot. Johnny's free hand settled on his windpipe and squeezed hard, cutting off the call for help at source. He squeezed harder, ignoring the blows his opponent aimed at his face, then flung him down with a curse. Horsemen were pushing their mounts through the undergrowth, and Johnny leapt on to his horse, confident now of escape. The half-breed was making strange croaking noises from where he lay, clutching his damaged throat, and the gunman doubted whether any of the others had the ability to follow him in the dark.

A few minutes later, having secured his horse out of earshot, he was back! As he'd half expected the rustlers hadn't even bothered to give chase. Too afraid or perhaps too sensible to follow a man who'd already proved his ability to shoot into a dark night over land where there was ample scope for an ambush. Not so the gunman! He was exactly where they'd least expect him, rifle in hand, watching them haul the beaten Indian to his feet.

The half-breed was barely able to croak an answer to his comrades' solicitous questions. He kept a grasp on his injured throat and spat out a mangled sentence that could have been a curse.

'Goddamn him.' One of the rustlers seemed to have taken command. 'He's damned near seen for Santos.' He stared at the Indian who was uttering some guttural noises which might have meant anything.

Apparently the half-breed also realized this for he held off from attempted speech and began to gesture at the forest around him. The inference was obvious and the rustlers stirred nervously.

'He'll be miles away by now,' one of them spoke optimistically. 'There's no one out there.' He paused uneasily. 'Is there?'

'Pick him up, lads.' Their leader gestured towards the

half-breed, drew his gun and began to back warily away from the trees. 'Get him up to the house and keep your eyes open.'

Johnny shifted his gun barrel forward. He could pick off a couple at least before they marked him down. He was almost ready to do it too, until his native caution took over. There were half a dozen on the spot and at least a score more within earshot. He'd go down fighting, but that would help no one.

He stayed silent and still under cover for several minutes after the rustlers had withdrawn, then slipped out to retrieve his knife which lay in full view. The pistol he'd lost proved harder to find, but at last he had it in his hands and began to creep back towards his horse. That scouts were still out was obvious to anyone with half an ear open, but with the half-breed, Santos, at least temporarily out of action, the gunman no longer had any fear of being detected.

# CHAPTER SIX

## PIETER

Johnny Royal rode back to the Rorovitz ranch in pensive mood. He felt he'd learned enough from his late night expedition to justify undertaking it. Trouble was, most of what he'd learned didn't seem to make any sense. Randy Nolan, and presumably therefore Jamie McKenzie too, were in with the rustlers up to their scrawny necks. But why did they need to be on hand at the McKenzie ranch? They seemed to give no aid in the rustling, which went on very well without them. Nolan was a gunhand, true, but he didn't seem to be particularly implicated in any gun play against McKenzie hands, nor would he have to stay at the ranch if that was his aim. Perhaps they intended to take over the ranch once old man McKenzie died? If so, they could do so without living on the premises.

Sarah! The gunman's lips pursed into a hard, angry line when he thought of her paired with the outlaw. If Nolan should marry her then he'd be the boss once the old man had breathed his last. That she feared and disliked Nolan would be no barrier to a man of his ilk. Johnny knew the type, and given a complaisant minister he'd force a wedding on her with no compunction whatsoever. Indeed, given the old man's state of health, why wait for his death? From what Barney had told him the local sheriff was unlikely to intervene without much more evidence of coercion than would be available. Barney and any other hand loyal enough to protest would be run off or worse!

Johnny damned the possibility. Why the hell should he care? But he did, and he damned himself too. He was as guilty as Nolan; even more guilty if the man did indeed intend marriage. Johnny knew he hadn't even considered that possibility until now. He'd set out to flirt, perhaps even seduce the girl. He cursed again. All his arguments were in vain; Randy Nolan had never meant to marry the girl, hadn't even tried to ingratiate himself with her. Given the right circumstances he'd force himself on her, perhaps as a precursor to murdering her. Would that leave Jamie as the rightful heir? Probably, but once again the vexing question remained. How would it help the rustlers?

He remembered the rustler chief's calm and measured, even cold, tones. Such a man as he wouldn't help Jamie to claim his lost inheritance without good reason, and good reason would only apply to something that served his own interests. He already had control of a ranch, what good would another do? He didn't want to work cattle, only to steal them! That Sarah was in serious danger once her grandfather died, Johnny sincerely believed, but he was still no closer to understanding why.

Perhaps it was the late hour, the tensions inevitable in a late night expedition against his enemies, exhaustion from the fight or his own dark thoughts that allowed him to let down his guard. In the light of events at the Flying T he should have been ready for anything, but he wasn't, and having stabled his mount he walked straight into the house suspecting nothing.

He knew he wasn't alone as soon as he walked through the door. In the deep gloom of the interior he could see no one, heard nothing that would alert him, but that extra sense essential to someone in his line of work kicked in and warned him. His muscles instinctively bunched and his gun leapt into his hand while he dropped to the floor, nervously rolling left and right before his unseen assailant could pinpoint his position.

Too late, as he already knew. If his unseen ambusher had wished to kill him, he'd have opened fire when he was silhouetted against the moonlight that flooded through the open door. Not Nolan then, not if he was on a mission to assassinate him. Santos perhaps? He'd have laid odds the half-breed Indian was out of the equation for the night, but it would be like him to stalk his foe through the dark rather than inflict a quick death by gunfire.

'Put your gun away, friend.'

Johnny tried to place the accent. It was slight, but none the less there. And despite the intruder's adoption of the word friend there was no indication of friendliness in his voice.

'Then we can talk.'

'Who are you?' Jonny made an abortive attempt to regain control of the situation.

'We talk first of who you are.'

'The name's Johnny Royal,' he admitted, still not putting up his pistol. 'I'm a ranch hand up at the McKenzie place.' He'd already realized his intruder had no connection with the rustlers, not those he'd seen tonight at any rate. Any one of them would already know his name, and his business also. He was no simple burglar either, no thief worth his salt would bother to attempt a robbery of Pieter's poor shack. So what did he want? And just where did he fit into the whole damned mess?

'I saw you with their foreman earlier,' the man admitted, 'but this is not the property of the McKenzie ranch. I hadn't looked to find you here.'

There was still no friendliness evident in the words, but neither was there animosity, and the gunman drew a faint hope from that. He suspected the other held a gun in his hands and knew exactly where he was, but evidently he wasn't going to shoot him out of hand. Neither did Johnny feel he was quite out of the woods just yet and he continued to aim his pistol squarely at the looming shadows from where the mystery man's voice emanated.

'The house belongs to a man called Pieter Rorovitz and I'm living here until he returns,' Johnny continued to answer the unspoken question, instinct telling him to stick to the plain unvarnished truth. 'He has a daughter who needs someone around to look after her.'

'Ah, sweet litttle Mariella, but she isn't here either.' Again a trace of that accent, and Johnny suddenly understood. The intruder knew the girl, presumably knew Pieter too. Perhaps even knew where Pieter was, or could make a guess more educated than his own.

'Mariella's up at the ranch. Sarah,' he paused, 'Miss McKenzie's looking after her for the night.'

'While you poke about the Flying T for her.' A match flared and a moment later the steady glare of an oil lamp illuminated the gaunt face of the intruder.

Johnny stared at his visitor in amazement. His face was freshly scarred and blood was still seeping from one of the wounds.

'I was at Miz Morrison's,' he explained, allowing the deadly muzzle of the shotgun he was holding to drop, 'in one of the back rooms. Her and I go back a long way and she was willing to hide me and bind up my wounds. I overheard the Flying T hands interrogate the girl you were with. From what she told them I assumed the Flying T ranch would be your next port of call.'

The gunman nodded while the stranger continued.

'You must be a brave man to make a strike at their lair alone. What did you learn from your foray?'

'Little enough,' Johnny admitted. 'I assumed the party at Miz Morrison's would continue for most of the night.' He grinned. 'I didn't count on them returning to the ranch to interrupt me.'

'Perhaps I know more than you, friend.' Again that word, with no more intimation of friendliness apparent in the tones of his voice. A state of armed neutrality had been entered, but no more than that.

'Then—' Johnny casually slipped his pistol into its holster and prepared to ask his own questions.

'What of the hands from the Flying T? Could they have followed you here?' The intruder interrupted him with a more urgent request and even in the dim light the gunman noted how his eyes flickered nervously towards the open doorway.

'No doubt they will in time, but not until they've licked their wounds.' Johnny gave an expurgated summary of events, before reminding the man of his own questions. 'You still haven't told me who you are.'

'My name is Pieter Rorovitz. I'm Mariella's father, or the closest she's got to one, at any rate.' The voice was warmer and the faint accent so evident in the harsher tones adopted earlier had almost disappeared, 'and for what it's worth, I own this sorry specimen of a ranch.' His eyebrows rose questioningly. 'I presume I have you to thank for the repairs and for looking out for my daughter?'

Pieter.' Johnny carefully measured the tall, slim figure. He himself was well over six foot, but the man topped him by an inch or two though that was not obvious while the man leaned heavily on the chair in front of him. He swayed awkwardly and staggered to a chair, crumpling into it.

'You're wounded!' The gunman darted forward and tore open Pieter's bloody shirt to reveal a ragged gunshot wound. There were other marks too: evidence of the lash and of the knife.

'They took me a few weeks ago,' explained Pieter. 'They asked me questions I had no answer to, despite their persuasive methods. I escaped a couple of days back, but took a bullet in my shoulder. It nearly did me in, for they had Santos on my track. He's their tame Indian tracker.'

'I know that particular half-breed myself,' returned the gunman. 'You must be a good scout if you evaded him.'

'I've escaped such men before,' replied Pieter, and went on to explain. 'My cousin and I fled our homes, evading the Cossack hordes that killed our families, and made our way to America together. Apart from him, Mariella is my only kin and I had to see if she was all right. Miz Morrison has agreed to look after her, but I was terrified they'd kidnapped her too.' His scarred and blood-stained face mirrored his terror. 'The girl is my constant joy and I couldn't bear the thought of her in their hands. Unlike most others, her love for me never needs to be bought.' There was a look of affection on the man's face that transformed it for a second and Johnny Royal guessed there was more to the story than he'd been told.

'What do you know?' The gunman suspected Pieter had no more leads than he himself, but he asked the question anyway. 'Why would a bunch of rustlers bother to kidnap you? What were they questioning you about?'

'I was never one to travel far,' Pieter began his story, apparently accepting Johnny as being trustworthy at last. 'Miz Morrison's place is about the furthest I'm likely to roam these days.'

'These days?' Johnny recognized the reservation in Pieter's words.

'I was still little more than a lad when I fetched up in the valley. James and I, the colonel's son, took up together. We were both young hot heads and took to raising Cain all over the territory.'

'James was disowned by his father,' Johnny reminded his visitor. He wasn't sure he wanted to know Pieter's life history, but since the man seemed to think it important, allowed the story to continue.

'He grew more wild every day. Soon there was a gang of us, with James as our undisputed leader. Whatever we did, he could top. Towards the end he was a terror, out of control, and I left him to his own devices. He turned into a killer at the last.' Pieter answered the unspoken question. 'He led a gang that waylaid the stage and shot it up. There wasn't much loot to be taken, but Judge Stone's daughter was one of the passengers.' He paused reflectively. 'Somehow the guard managed to escape and contact the sheriff. The posse lit out real quick, but when they found the stage, everyone in it was dead and the girl was missing. Her defiled and mutilated body was found two days later.'

'And James?'

'Everyone knew he was to blame, but there was no hard evidence against him. The guard was too scared to testify and the gang had scattered to the four winds. I'll swear the colonel knew though. The old man wouldn't hand his own son over to the law, too proud of his own good name, but he flung him off the ranch and never spoke his name again.'

'Were you a part of the gang that day?'

'No, I'd long since stopped riding with the scum he'd brought together,' replied Pieter. 'He asked me to follow him into exile, told me we could live like kings. I refused.' Pieter laughed out loud. 'You never could fathom what he'd do next. God alone knows where he got the money from, probably a pay-off from his father, but he bought up this here ranch for me. It never was much of a place, but I set to work building it up, until Elena arrived. She was the most beautiful thing I ever saw, and a girl in trouble to boot. She wouldn't have looked twice at me otherwise. Mariella was born a few months later, and within a year her mother was on her travels once more. Took off after a gambler and broke my heart. I didn't take much interest in the ranch after that, but I've always looked after Mariella real good.' His eyes misted over. 'She's the image of her mother.'

'You never saw James again then?'

'Four, maybe five years back the bank in Boulder was

robbed. There was gold bullion there, a special shipment from the mine. The folk in town always reckoned James was in on it, but they had no real proof, not anything they could swear to in a court of law. No one would admit he actually saw James's face among the raiders.' A shadow crossed the tired and grimy face in front of the gunman. 'Getting the gold loaded was a long job, plenty of time to raise a posse, and they had to shoot their way out of town. Jess Logan was sheriff at the time, and he and a couple of his deputies were killed in the crossfire. The outlaws lost men too, and James reckoned he was the only one to escape.'

'He *was* involved then. What about you?' Johnny was sure the story had a point and that Pieter would come to it.

'No, I wasn't involved, not in the raid itself, but I was implicated in the aftermath. James was fatally wounded, but he somehow managed to make his way to the ranch here for assistance. I could see he was close to death when he staggered in. I didn't know what he'd done then, not that it would have mattered. I did what I could for him. He was shot full of holes and raving in some sort of delirium.'

'So Campbell McKenzie's son finally died here?'

'No. I knew I couldn't risk the doctor in case there was a hue and cry out, so I went to fetch Colonel McKenzie. He knew what had happened – he'd been in town himself. Knew what it meant, too! He may have disinherited James, but he wouldn't allow any son of his to be hauled off to jail. James died in the family home and took the location of his latest haul with him, though I didn't know it then.'

'Didn't he tell you?' The gunman's eye's searched Pieter face for any sign of a lie. 'You were his friend.'

'No, he was virtually unconscious by the time he reached me and there was no sign of any gold. In retrospect, I suppose I should have guessed. James had made his escape in a buckboard, not the most convenient of vehicles for a fleeing man, but if I gave it any thought at the time, maybe I'd have put it down to his injuries. He was in no state to ride.'

'Did no one ever suspect?'

'A posse arrived at the ranch a day or two later and gave it the once-over. With the sheriff and most of his deputies dead, raising enough men to give chase took time. There was nothing here to suspect by that time. Besides, they knew James never gave anything to anyone if he could help it. Anyhow, I'd never had more than a dollar or two to my name, and they knew if I had the stolen cache, I'd have been raising Cain down at Miz Morrison's every night.'

'The gold was never recovered. It must have occurred to you later that he may have hidden it.'

'Surprisingly enough, no. I guess I assumed one of the others escaped too, in good enough shape to take the gold with him. Good enough assumption as it happens. One of them had escaped, but without the gold.' He stared hard at the gunman. 'There are visitors on the McKenzie ranch.'

'His grandson, James's son.' Johnny decided the pieces were beginning to settle into place. 'Got a gunman there too, Randy Nolan.'

'That's the one. He came around with the gang a time or two, questioning me. I couldn't help him, even if I'd wanted to.'

'Mariella reckons there're bogeymen about; she's terrified of them. Are they the men she means?'

'Most likely.' Pieter looked worried. 'Have they been back?'

'Just the two of them, far as I know. She took to sleeping out before I came along.'

'Thank God! They took me off to the Flying T a couple of weeks back, and I've been scared stiff they'd take her too.'

'She's safe enough for now, but I'll get Sarah to arrange a berth in town for her until this business is settled.'

'I'd appreciate it.'

'It's getting late, I can fix a meal before bed if you like.' Johnny Royal decided Pieter had nothing more to say on the matter, and made the offer assuming he intended to stay.

'I'll take the food, but I won't stay overnight.' A lop-sided smile flashed fleetingly across Pieter's face. 'Just in case the Flying T decide to pay a visit.' He stared hard at the gunman. 'I'd advise you to do the same.'

# CHAPTER SEVEN

# THE COLONEL'S LAIR

The following morning Johnny Royal made his way up to the McKenzie house early and knocked sharply on the kitchen door. There'd been no further sign of Pieter, but he suspected the man couldn't be far away.

'Johnny.' Sarah greeted him coolly, but there was a sparkle in her eye that hinted she wasn't displeased to see him. 'Do you want some breakfast, or shall I take you straight up to Grandpa.'

'The condemned man's already eaten,' he replied ruefully, not at all sure he wanted to see the old man, let alone talk to him. What the devil would they have to talk about? Nothing, so far as he could see! Or was his burgeoning relationship with Sarah to become the subject? Did the colonel have the notion some common ranch hand was romancing his granddaughter to inherit the ranch? If so, from all he'd heard of the old man's fiery temper, no doubt he'd be blasted out of the room and his

76

job in quick succession.

'Don't be so silly, Grandpa will love you. He likes to put on a show, but he's a darling really.' Sarah crooked a finger at him and led the way deeper into the house, eventually ascending a back stairway that Johnny was sure the old man would never have used. She obviously recognized this herself, but excused the route. 'Jamie and his friend aren't usually up this early, but you never know, and I don't want them to chance upon you.' She paused a moment while she negotiated a particularly narrow doorway, before adding with transparent honesty. 'Especially up here, where they may suspect you of becoming Grandpa's ally.'

'They've already come visiting.' Johnny grunted, keeping his reply to the bare facts. 'We had a long talk.'

Sarah stopped dead and threw him the sort of speaking look over her shoulder that made him wish he hadn't divulged the information. 'What did they want to talk to you about?'

'This and that,' Johnny replied casually. 'Your secret engagement to Nolan, for instance.'

'My what?' Sarah hissed, then grinned when she saw the look on his face. 'You're funning me, what did they really want with you?'

'No, truly. You're to marry young Nolan as soon as your grandpa's out of the way, but you don't want anyone to know just yet in case the old man takes against the lad. And him such a catch in the marriage mart.' He tried to look crestfallen. 'A story that touched my heart, and there you were last night, leading me on in a manner that can only be described as brazen.'

'How dare they!' There were storm clouds brewing in the girl's eyes and she refused to be led off the scent by his jocular manner. 'Did they try to get you off the ranch?'

'They might have mentioned my retirement,' he replied. No point in worrying the girl with their threats, especially since he intended to ignore them. 'Not that I'm likely to leave now I've seen the way your hips move under that dress. You'll have to lead me up the back stairs more often.'

Sarah gasped at his audacity and he could have sworn she was blushing.

'Doing it deliberately to entrap me I shouldn't wonder. For shame, and you almost a married woman.'

'Johnny Royal.' The girl turned to face him with her hands on her hips. 'You won't put me off the scent, so I warn you.'

'Nothing happened,' he admitted quietly. 'They evidently sensed my interest in you and told me the tale. Suggested I move on.'

'And are you interested in me?'

'Nothing much else to do around here,' Johnny teased her, but his gaze held a different message and she continued up the stairway satisfied, the heat in her cheeks measuring the rhythmic sway of her hips, which she made no attempt to abate.

'Grandpa,' she opened an ornate wooden door without knocking, her eyes anxiously piercing through the gloom in the room beyond. 'I've brought Mr Royal here to see you.'

'Royal?' Johnny recognized the testy inflexion of an invalid who remembered all too vividly what it was like to be active. 'Darned fellow took long enough to introduce himself. What sort of hand is he anyway? Damned if I like you taking on cowmen without my say so.'

'I took advice from Barney, Grandpa.' There was a softening of Sarah's voice when she spoke to the old man, but she was grinning and evidently not at all overawed by his blustering.

'He's as big a fool as you are, but you'd better send the fellow in.' Colonel McKenzie barked gruffly, but it was obvious to the gunman that despite his attempt at irritation there was real love between the pair. 'You can go away and leave us, lass. I'll have no petticoats interfering in our dealings, good or bad. If the man can't speak for himself, I'll have no truck with him, good cowman or not.'

Johnny nodded at Sarah and strode confidently into the room. The old man was laid out on the bed, propped into a sitting position with well stuffed pillows. Campbell McKenzie had evidently been a big man, perhaps as tall as he himself, and broad to match. The vigour and strength that was still evident in his eyes had ebbed from his body, presumably from his affliction, the aftermath of which had left him gaunt and hollow-faced. He was pale, his breathing forced and shallow for such a large frame, but there was a glitter in his eye that showed his spirit had still not left him. Johnny had no difficulty in seeing why, even in his current distressed state, the rustlers didn't want to face him down in his own home when all they had to do was wait for him to die.

'Johnny Royal, sir.' The gunman shook off his grim thoughts, held out his hand and strode across to the bed. The colonel flapped his left hand awkwardly and Johnny rapidly switched hands to shake it. He found the grip unexpectedly firm despite the pale emaciation of a hand that had once worked as hard as any of his men. The old man's right arm lay uselessly on the coverlets, evidently paralysed in the aftermath of his seizure.

'Pleased to meet you,' Johnny continued in lieu of anything else to say.

'Damned if I know why.' The colonel may have been laid low, but there was still an echo of strength in his voice.

'Damned if I know that either,' the gunman admitted. He'd already realized the old man wouldn't be taken in by any foolish attempt to pander to him. 'I'm not the first man your granddaughter's taken on while you've been lying abed. Did you insist on seeing all the others?'

'None of them lasted long enough. Barney didn't like them neither.'

'He likes me?' Johnny's eyebrows rose.

'You know damned well he does,' the old man replied testily. 'So does Sarah, though I'll not have her bothered by any old wastrel just because he's good with a gun.' The fire in his eyes suddenly dimmed and Campbell McKenzie looked just what he was. A sick, weak, old man close to death. 'Don't play with her affections. She'll be all alone when I go.'

'You'll—'

'Damn you, don't play the fool with me. I'm dying and I know it as well as anyone. The ranch should belong to Sarah, but it's about played out unless she can find a man strong enough to back her.' He paused a moment. 'He'll have to be ruthless too.' The old man stared at Johnny for several long, uncomfortable moments, measuring his resolve, then nodded. 'You're ruthless enough if you've a mind, I'll be bound, but do you love the chit?'

'We've barely had time to get acquainted,' Johnny protested. Then took stock of the situation. 'Yes,' he admitted, as much to himself as to the old man. Sarah was the only reason he was staying put.

'You'll have to face down that fool of a grandson of mine,' warned Campbell McKenzie, then laughed out loud. 'Easy meat for a man like you, but I'll wager his black-hearted friend won't be so readily moved.'

'I thought you weren't to be told about them,' Johnny grinned admiringly at the old man.

'Damned fools. I make it my business to know what's going on in my own house. Can't do anything about it, though.' The old man gestured at his useless body and cursed. 'I'd only stir up a parcel of trouble for other folks to clear up.' He paused reflectively. 'Damned if I know why they're here, either. Young Jamie might have come to make his peace, not that he's ever tried to do anything of the sort, but his partner's a different breed altogether. He's here for a reason, and it isn't for a share in the ranch when I'm dead and buried. I'll lay odds he's never done an honest day's work in his life and neither does he intend to do one in the future.' The old man subsided deeper into his pillows. 'Got his eye on Sarah too, but only to ruin her.' He laughed weakly when Johnny stiffened. 'Likely you'll take a deal of moving too, but watch your back around him, he's the sort of sidewinder who'd find a bushwhacking easy.'

'They're after the gold?' Johnny surprised the old man. Surprised himself too, he hadn't meant to bring the subject up.

'Gold? What gold?' Campbell McKenzie eased himself slowly forward. 'What do you know?' he asked suspiciously.

'I know your son was brought here after his final raid.'

'You do, do you?' The colonel's voice raised menacingly, then fell back just as suddenly, his face visibly paler. 'Are you a lawman?' he inquired.

'No, I'm not. Nor do I have any interest in your son; or his ill-gotten gains either, come to that.'

'Just as well.' The old man stared at him fixedly. 'Suppose you tell me just what you do know and how you happen to know it.'

'The bank was robbed in Boulder. Your son was shot. Somehow he ended up at the Rorovitz place where Pieter took him in. He wasn't safe there, though; everyone knew that he and Pieter went back years. So he ended up coming to you for help. There were townsfolk shot, some dead, including the sheriff himself, but eventually there'd be a posse. You were an important man in the valley, they'd believe your denials, like they wouldn't Pieter's, and on such a large ranch what did it matter if they did institute a search. You'd always be a step or two ahead of them.'

'How?' The old man's face had sunken further, and he looked closer to death than ever.

'Pieter came to visit last night. He told me all he knew.' Johnny Royal didn't embellish the story, but he kept his eyes on the old man who seemed to have sunk into his own memories of the past.

'You're right,' Campbell McKenzie confirmed at last. 'Pieter brought him. I kept it quiet, of course. Sarah has no idea James ever came back, however short his visit. If I'd known then how many he'd killed maybe I'd have handed him over, son or no son, but without the sheriff to hassle them the posse didn't set out for several days and James was dead and buried by that time. Died in a matter of hours, still cursing me.'

The old colonel's head drooped and he sank back into his memories. 'James and Pieter always were close,' he began in strangely reminiscent tone. 'Stuck together through thick and thin; always in some trouble or other, the pair of them. Didn't pay it much mind. I was wild myself when I was young and I had the ranch to manage. Took me years to build it up; a lot of hard work and no time for family life. It wasn't until much later I realized he was worse than wild. I should have reined him in, but by then it was too late.' The old man stared hard at Johnny. 'I wasn't much of a father, Mr Royal. I had a temper too. One day he went too far and we fought.' There was a tear in the old man's eye. 'I beat him to the ground. My own son!' For a moment there was silence in the room. 'I might have saved him even then, but I was too proud, too full of my own importance. He left and went to the dogs. If there was any dirty deed that boy wouldn't do, I've never heard of it, so I disowned him.'

A flash of the old man's fiery temper reared. 'If his snivelling son and that misbegotten dog he brought with him are expecting to find anything here they'll be out of luck though. James never had the gold. Not with him.'

'Not with him?'

'I didn't give it a thought at the time. I know the bank never recovered the gold, but it didn't occur to me that a man as badly wounded as James could have safely hidden it.'

'You said, not with him,' prompted Johnny again. 'Are you suggesting he might have stashed it away, or given it to Rorovitz?'

'He'd never have trusted Pieter, or anyone else for that matter, not with anything of value.'

'Perhaps another gang member?'

'Not likely! James would have trusted his own men even less. There's no honour amongst the murdering bunch of thieves he consorted with. He'd have escaped with the gold in his charge all right, must have done. I thought it was the doctor himself come visiting when they first rolled in. Afterwards Pieter told me how James had arrived at the ranch in Doc's buckboard with a saddle horse tied up behind. Funny way to escape a posse when he could have travelled far faster on the horse.'

'It was full of gold?'

'Not then, but it may have been before he went to Pieter for help.' The colonel's eyes lit up as his brain began to work. 'He was filthy, not good earth like he'd just dug it up, but grimy and grey. Course he'd probably been rolling around a good deal while he was escaping and later, when he went to earth.' The colonel stared at at the gunman as though he were a fellow conspirator. 'It would have been at least a day after the raid before he sought Pieter's help.'

'You know where he hid the loot.' Johnny made the accusation. 'You've always known.'

'Maybe.' Campbell McKenzie wasn't going to play any more games. 'I recognized the dirt even then. James used to play up in the old Indian caves. He discovered them, told me about them ages before he went wrong. They run for miles under the hills, full of bones and old cave paintings. Guess it was an earlier race from the Indians that were around when I arrived. I never did see the paintings myself; he was secretive even in those days. Far as I know, he was the only one that ever knew their exact location.'

The old man stared into space a moment, then went on with his tale. 'Didn't dawn on me at first. Not that he'd hidden his cache there. I thought he'd just gone to ground and only risked the trip to Pieter when he realized how bad he was shot. I didn't even connect it with the caves when I heard the gold he'd stolen was still missing. It could have been anywhere.' A spasm of pain shook him. 'Maybe I didn't want to think about it. James was never seen; what people didn't know couldn't blacken the family name any further. Don't matter why no more, I kept it well out of mind until the last few days.

'You get a lot of time to think in my condition, Mr Royal. When I heard Pieter was gone I suddenly realized he must know about the caves as well. Wondered if he'd suddenly put the pieces together and gone and got the gold for himself.'

'Would he have left Mariella? Even for gold.'

'No, Mr Royal. I already realized that myself. He'd have taken her with him, or at least arranged someone to take her in. He was a wastrel and a scoundrel, but the only good thing he ever did in this life was look after that girl.'

The colonel reflected again. 'You're right about the gold. I probably knew for ages before I even admitted it to myself. James hid the loot. In the caves, maybe even elsewhere.' He paused. 'Jamie or that thug he has with him, knew all about it. They've tracked him down and taken Pieter. Probably thought he knew more than he does. Maybe they believe it's hidden somewhere on the ranch even now.' He suddenly looked up. The door had been left open a little and a shadow had moved behind it.

'Who's there?'

Johnny Royal lost no time. He'd had his back to the door and seen nothing, but he'd watched the colonel's eyes flicker and the gun was in his hands before he was halfway across the room. He stared down the corridor baffled. No one was in sight, but there was a hint of cigarette smoke in the air.

'Well!' The testy inquiry came from the bed, but Johnny could only shrug his shoulders.

'They heard. That worthless grandson of mine, or his tame gunslinger, doesn't matter which. They heard.'

'Probably.' Johnny tested the air with his nose again. It was a distinctive scent. He didn't know which of the men

85

smoked those cigarettes, but whoever it was had passed the room in the last few minutes. 'Who else knows about those caves?'

'No one but James, far as I know. He came across them by accident; told me the entrance was hidden and no one else would ever discover them. Pieter may have gone with him, but I never heard that. They won't be easy to find. I've ridden every inch of this valley in the last forty years and never found a trace of them, not that I was looking.'

'Sort of thing a father might tell his children about.' Johnny gave the old man a searching look when he returned to the bedside.

'Not James.' Campbell McKenzie gave a snort of disgust. 'He never owned a shred of paternal instinct.'

'He had a son, at least.'

'His mother was some floozie back East. Died of drink and too many men. James at least had the decency to take the lad in.'

'You know a lot about James, considering you disowned him.' Johnny made the accusation quietly, knowing the old man would fire up over such a personal thing, but in the event he was surprised.

'Campbell told me. He was my eldest; never wild, never did anything wrong in his entire life.' It sounded like an accusation, and the old man went on to confirm it. 'Used to think he was the spineless one, but I soon found out he was no such thing. He was a fine boy, a son to be proud of. He put his head down and worked harder than anyone I knew.' He grinned. 'Only one that ever dared to contradict me to my face, too. Oh, James would disobey me, but he'd never face me direct. Sarah does too, she's a credit to her father.'

'Her mother too.'

'Her mother too,' concurred the old man. 'Never really knew her, though we met at the wedding. Campbell went East to study at college – that's when he met James again. He married there, she died, and he returned with Sarah in tow.'

The room went quiet for several minutes and just as Johnny thought the old man had gone to sleep and stirred to leave the room, the colonel spoke again.

'I'd like the gold returned to the bank, Mr Royal. I lost a lot of friends over the robbery. No one could directly accuse James, because he was never found. Dead or alive. But it's been a stain on the family name. There's folk in town still won't talk to me or mine. Don't care for myself, but I do for Sarah.'

'I'll look, Mr McKenzie.' Johnny Royal suddenly felt sorry for the old man. He was a proud man, and his son had dragged the family name in the mire. He suddenly felt sick. Hadn't he done just the same to his own folk? Well, at last he could do something for someone else. Campbell McKenzie or Sarah? He wasn't going to allow himself to answer that question.

'You won't find those caves yourself. Not in the time we've got left,' the colonel told him. There was a wild light in his eyes and a flush on his cheeks. It was a time for action and the old war horse was fretting at the reins. He couldn't act himself, but he could still pull the strings. 'You've been ordered up into the hills to ride the line. No need to tell anyone but Barney, but there's a line hut way out on the bluffs. Sort of place the caves are likely to be, and if you're right and Jamie knows about them, he'll take off that way. Keep an eye on him and he may lead you directly to the cache. Leave right away, or you'll miss him. Now be off with you, you've tired me!'

# CHAPTER EIGHT

# THE CAVES

As soon as she realized Johnny had left her grandfather, Sarah led him through a dingy corridor behind the kitchen to a small room he'd never seen before. It was furnished as an office and she quickly explained its purpose.

'No one will interrupt us here,' she began. 'I doubt Jamie or his friend even know it exists. For certain they've never shown any interest in the running of the ranch or its accounts.' She looked at him expectantly. 'You were a long time with Grandpa? What happened?'

Johnny had been thinking on his feet. How much should he tell Sarah? She'd very probably have her own ideas on the way to proceed, unlikely to agree with those he and her grandfather had agreed.

'He asked about you and me,' he temporized, then realized if he was to have any sort of relationship with the girl, he'd have to tell the truth and spill the entire story. 'Then he told me all about your uncle.'

'James? Then he knows Jamie is here?'

'Has done since they arrived, I suspect. He may be sick, but his brain's still active and I dare say he has his own methods of staying in touch.'

'Why talk about James? He hasn't seen him in twenty years.'

'You may not realize it but your uncle died here a few years back following a bank robbery in Boulder.' Johnny looked her steadily in the eye, trying to assess her state of mind. 'Your grandfather thought it best to keep that news secret.'

'I remember everyone blaming James at the time,' returned the girl hotly, 'but I thought they were just guessing, condemning my uncle because of his reputation. I never realized it was actually true. What happened? Did Grandpa shield him from the law?'

'I gather he died before your grandfather had to make that decision. It also appears he may have secreted the proceeds of the robbery close by.'

'Then Grandpa knows where it is. How exciting!'

'He's speculating,' Johnny told her shortly, 'but it explains the mystery of Pieter's disappearance.'

'To hunt for the gold?' Sarah frowned in concentration. 'If he knew, why would he have waited this long before starting the search?'

'I imagine he would have done so long ago if he had any inkling where it was. As it is, he was kidnapped and taken over to the Flying T for questioning. He only managed to engineer his escape a few days back, which no doubt explains why Jamie and his tame gunslinger, Nolan, have been so interested in Pieter's ranch in the past couple of days.'

'How do you know?'

'Pieter dropped by last night. He was really after Mariella, fears the gang might plan to abduct her too, but fortunately she was safe with you.'

'Why fortunately?'

'He'd have taken her and disappeared most likely, leaving us with no clue to what's happening. He's running scared of this bunch, with good reason too, it seems. Can you see she's kept safe? Not here, not with Nolan in residence. Someone in town perhaps.'

'I'll see to it,' declared Sarah, 'but there's something else. Something you haven't told me.'

'Your grandfather believes James may have hidden the gold in some caves, but he doesn't know their location.' Johnny went on to tell the girl the whole of his conversations with her grandfather.

'There's a whole lot of caves in the neighbourhood,' Sarah corroborated slowly. 'It could lie hidden in any one of them.'

'This one's different. Decorated with paintings on the wall. Done by some sort of extinct Indian tribe from what your grandfather believes.'

'I've never heard of any caves like that around here.'

'Seems like James kept the secret to himself. Perhaps he had a reason. Maybe he used this cave to hide stolen goods long before the bullion robbery.' Although the gunman had no more than conjecture to go on, he considered this explanation was only too likely.

'I assume you're off to search for this cave.'

'Not exactly.' Johnny hesitated a moment before plunging on. 'One or both of your guests passed the room while we were talking. I don't know if they heard anything of any note.' His voice trailed off.

'They must have been listening.' Sarah was certain of her facts. 'I deliberately boarded them in the other wing. If they were outside Grandpa's door, they were there for a purpose. Are you sure?'

'I smelt the smoke. One of them smokes a perfumed cigarette, probably foreign.'

'Nolan.' Sarah spoke shortly. 'They stink the house out sometimes. But what of it? Even if they did overhear, they won't know where the cave lies, any more than you do.'

'Jamie is James's son.' Johnny's suspicions seemed ridiculous in the cold light of day, but not so ridiculous as to be discounted.

'So you're going to trail them.' Sarah laughed, but there was no humour in her eyes. 'Grandpa's idea, I'll be bound.' She pursed her lips defiantly. 'I'll go and have a word with him. You've already done enough for this family.'

'No, Sarah.' Johnny stepped in, his mind as set as hers. 'I've done too much in my lifetime I'm not proud to acknowledge. Helping return gold bullion to the bank will lay a lot of my demons too. Not that there's any danger. So far as they're concerned I'm off riding the line and as soon as I've discovered the location of this cave, I'll be riding into town to inform the sheriff.'

'No gunplay.' Sarah eyed him suspiciously.

'Not if I can help it.'

It was later that morning when Johnny Royal rode out of the ranch, freshly provisioned, and heading into the hills in search of the line hut he'd been allocated as temporary accommodation. Neither Jamie nor Randy had set off as yet, but inquiries soon elicited the information that they'd asked the cook for rations enough for two or three days so they could explore the surrounding countryside. The gunman wasn't yet sure whether their patient approach to cave hunting was due to knowing where it was, or in trying to guess where it might be. One thing he was sure of, Nolan had been listening and must surely be set on locating the cave.

It was a difficult decision, but Johnny made straight for the line hut. It was close enough to the bluffs to form a convenient headquarters and, moreover, it offered a small barn in which to stable his horse. He could have hobbled it somewhere off the trail, but it might have given him away, or worse, be left out in the sun all day and unable to perform when needed.

He strode back down the trail to the bluffs. It was only three or four miles, but his boots weren't made for walking and he soon began to doubt the wisdom of his decision. Nevertheless, he trudged on until he reached the point where the trail began to climb into the hills, and there he stopped to survey the lie of the land. In all probability, he considered, the cave would open on to a cliff, but which one? His keen eyes scoured the bleak, rocky hills but, finding no clues, he eventually settled on a scramble high into a rocky eyrie from which he could easily keep a look-out over a wide swathe of the surrounding countryside. And there he settled down to wait.

It was late into the afternoon before his quarry appeared, by which time he'd almost given them up. Either they had as little idea as he where the cave was, or it was situated in some other hills, and though he was prepared to wait until nightfall his guard had relaxed, allowing him to doze off in the heat of the sun. Consequently they were almost upon him before he saw them, leaving him in a bit of a quandary. Should he attempt to keep them in sight on foot, or go collect his horse.

The faint line that made up the trail ran close alongside the cliffs at this point, and he let that drive his final decision to continue on foot. The cave must be close by, had to lie close to the trail; if all their surmises were correct then a dying man had driven a buckboard loaded with heavy gold bullion right up to its entrance.

Less than half an hour passed before he began to doubt his decision. Not only was his own progress slowed by the rock-strewn slopes he'd chosen, but the trail was beginning to curve away, and though his quarry was riding at no more than walking pace, they were already beginning to leave him in their wake. Evidence of several caves had been passed, but none had gained the least interest from the men he pursued. He took hope that this was an indication of Jamie's knowledge of his destination, but was left wondering if he'd been mistaken in abandoning his horse when Jamie suddenly pointed towards a particularly prominent cliff.

It was a sheer, almost vertical mass of rock that stood out from the rocky faces around it, and the first indication they might be nearing their destination. Jamie pointed again, towards the rock-strewn shale slopes that shrouded the lower slopes of the cliff and Johnny began to scan the area impatiently. If the lad could see any evidence of a cave, then he was a better man than he.

In fact the gunman found himself so engrossed in the search for a cave that he almost missed the disappearance of his quarry. They'd lightly hobbled their horses, unloaded rope and what looked like bundles of sticks, and set out into the jumble of rock, melting into the landscape almost immediately. Johnny stared and at last caught sight of a head appearing briefly between boulders before he set out to regain the trail and follow them.

Finding the position from which they'd disappeared was easy enough – he had only to make for their horses, who looked up suspiciously when he appeared. He paused, stiff with worry in case their restlessness betrayed him, but they quickly decided he represented no threat and went back to grazing contentedly on what little sparse vegetation survived precariously on the edge of the trail. There was a narrow gap between two huge boulders adjacent and he drew his pistol before warily squeezing through its dark maw.

At first he thought he was actually within a cavern, for the roof was completely sealed over and it grew steadily darker, finally ending in a sheer rock face. There were no side turnings, and for a moment he was perplexed, until he remembered the brief view of someone's head. He stared up at the high ceiling while he slowly retraced his steps and eventually found what he wanted. Someone's boot had recently scored the rock above his head, and by straining his eyes he could see there was a narrow gap through which a man could squeeze.

In fact, by the time he'd successfully clambered up to it, he found the gap was easily wide enough, but all it led to was a narrow path between boulders on the hillside. His booted feet slipped easily in the shale and he had to pick his way with care in case the rattle of stones should alert the men ahead of him. On the other hand, it was a simple matter to track his quarry for the disturbed path was easy to see, a bonus when there were several side paths to lure the unwary. Jamie and Nolan had evidently found the same problem, for some of these had been entered and then discarded. For a moment he abandoned his perusal of their trail and looked up instead. The vertical mass of rock Jamie had earlier pointed out loomed above him, evidently the guide they were following.

The trail ended abruptly. Paths led off in several different directions, but the tell-tale scuff marks in the shale had disappeared. Johnny scanned the sheer cliff face anxiously, without being any the wiser until he spotted the peg driven into the shale almost at his feet. Strong twine had been attached, a guide rope that led through the narrowest of fissures, hidden by boulders and seemingly leading directly into the ground. He lay down and thrust his head through the hidden gap. It was like some sort of narrow vent hole, falling vertically for several feet. A cautious investigation by hand showed that precarious steps were cut into the stone like a ladder. At the bottom a curious flickering glow lit up the floor, and he realized Jamie and Nolan were far better prepared than he. Presumably, the bundles of twigs they'd unloaded had been twined into a improvised torch.

Satisfied they were deep underground, he cautiously lowered himself down the vent, utilizing what he could of the narrow ledges cut at intervals, only to find himself in a much larger cave that led deeper into the mountain. The faint glow ahead had almost disappeared, but the tough twine guide was easy to follow even in the dark, and he set off in its wake. The going was easier now they were in the cave, but he had to concede a greater respect for Jamie's outlaw father. He must have been tough as old boots to have hauled the stolen gold over this distance, a heavy enough load for anyone, let alone a man already fatally wounded. Evidently, he had inherited some of the grit and strength of his father, even if he'd used it in a less than noble cause.

The cave suddenly opened up into a vast cavern, leaving his quarry easily visible in the light of their torches. They were striding along a vast table of almost flat rock, searching every nook and cranny they came to, and Johnny immediately took cover behind a nearby rock formation. The light reflected eerily around the cavern, here and there picking out rocky walls fantastically painted with scenes of long-gone life: hunting; the campfire; and animals of every description. The pair engaged in the search didn't seem to notice any of this. Their attention was on the ground around them, and they seemed to be moving in some sort of search pattern that took them to and fro in front of the gunman's own position. In the far distance some chance ray of light reflected on the surface of a vast lake, perhaps even a slow flowing underground river. It was towards this the pair began to gravitate, until Jamie darted forward with a cry of joy.

On the floor, quite open to anyone with light available, lay a number of slim boxes which evidently concealed the gold. Both of the men ran across and began to jerk at the fastenings of one. It was evidently not locked, for they threw back the lid with little or no trouble, and stared at the contents. Johnny was too far away to see exactly what was inside, but the look of awe on their faces told him everything. They'd found the gold!

He watched while they picked out a couple of heavy

bars that glinted in the light of their torches while they displayed them with due reverence. The hum of conversation reached him with renewed sharpness; they were evidently arguing together, although to what purpose he couldn't imagine. Their voices, flung against the rocky floor and echoing walls, reached him in a dizzying staccato of meaningless sounds through which no more than a few amounted to sensible words. Nevertheless, he got the impression Nolan was suggesting they shared the loot between themselves, while Jamie sensibly wanted to inform the remainder of the outlaws. Johnny realized Jamie trusted his erstwhile friend as little as he himself would have done. Once the gold had been carried from the chamber and they'd escaped, there would be nothing to hold Nolan in check.

Be that as it may, and whatever the outcome, the gold had to stay in the cavern for now. They could take out a few ingots, but their two horses would be unequal to the massive weight of a haul like this. A wagon or a string of pack horses would be needed to ferry the gold in any quantity.

Johnny ducked low while the pair, still arguing, passed by on the way to the entrance. He stayed in hiding until the last glimmer of their torches had disappeared and set off to search for the gold himself.

Despite knowing exactly where it lay, he found the task of locating it extremely difficult in the dark and he barked his shins on several occasions before he blundered into the low-lying boxes. That the pair would be back to collect the gold he didn't doubt for a moment, with or without their colleagues. And that would be the end of the matter. They'd escape scot free, an eventuality he had no intention of allowing. Not only had he promised the colonel a chance to clear the family name, but too many men had already died for that gold.

He sat down and set to, planning his campaign. A vision of the nearby lake slowly formed and he began to edge cautiously in its direction. The darkness was absolute and he took especial care not to blunder into the water. The edge was sudden, almost vertical, and he took the time to reach into his clothing for a match. The sudden flare seared his eyes, and though he held the short taper until the flames bit into his fingers all he could see was the black water receding into the distance. Temporarily disorientated by the returning darkness he lay down and dangled one arm into the freezing depths, but was only able to ascertain its depth by extending his reach so far as to submerge his shoulders. He shivered and drew back; was this the best he could do?

In the dark he soon realized it was, and felt his way blindly back to the boxes. He lit another of his dwindling supply of matches, and soon found all the boxes had been opened, and when he tried lifting one, he realized why. He could barely move the box on his own and a wounded James would have had no chance of completing a task that involved moving several of the heavily packed boxes. A thought came to him and he began to lift the ingots separately, leaving the boxes in place. The gold he slowly and laboriously transferred to the lake, and the boxes he left, filled with heavy rock of which there was a plentiful supply. He had no doubt the outlaws would open the boxes when they returned, but it was worth taking a further chance to slow them down.

Feeling he'd left a job well done, he began to make his

way slowly across the cavern back to the cave he'd entered by. His heart lurched into his mouth when he realized there was no twine to guide him. He struck another match and searched further, finding a second cave leading out of the cavern, and with mounting desperation a third. Shaking off a feeling of hopelessness he began to search more methodically, using up the remainder of his matches well before he'd finished, only to find that several caves led into the huge cavern he was in. None of them contained the twine, and realizing Jamie and Nolan must have taken it back with them, he sat down to think.

# CHAPTER NINE

# IN THE CAVERN

How long he sat before the chilling knowledge that he was lost fully enveloped him, he was never afterwards quite sure. It was the still drip of water that first alerted him to the facts. The sound of water dripping had echoed in hollow cadence around the main chamber, but it hadn't rung out quite so loudly or insistently. A sudden presentiment caused him to stagger to his feet and reach high over his head, searching for confirmation that he was still safely ensconced in the familiar arena of the main cavern. His heart lurched when his questing finger tips traced the ragged rocky outline of the roof.

Don't panic, he told himself immediately, thrusting down the sick dread that crawled out of his vitals, spawned by the velvet darkness and the cruel aknowledgement of his predicament. It's dark, he told himself, and you're too close to the edge of the chamber. Yes, that was it. He attempted to rationalise his fears, tried to convince himself the ceiling must angle down sharply by the wall.

He felt for the rocky mass at his back, reached out and staggered forward blindly, almost immediately hitting rock again. He strove to edge around it, tried to tell himself it was only a boulder in his path, but was soon forced to admit it was another wall, in a tunnel that seemed to lead on forever. Reality struck with stunning force; he was truly lost. Lost in the dark, somewhere in the sprawling maze of caves that ran under the bluffs. Somehow he'd exited the main cavern and stumbled into some side alley that led off it. Panic began to well up again, paralysing his mind, until he forced himself to think logically, trying to imagine the direction from which he'd come, how long he'd been walking, when he could have lost the main cavern.

Not long, he told himself. Too long, his inner conscience argued. How far had he wandered? Not far, he told himself hopefully. He couldn't have walked any distance from the main cavern! Too far, his conscience repeated, and this time he had to agree with it. The passing of time was difficult to assess in the dark, but it must have been at least an hour since he'd run out of matches to strike and he could have covered a fair distance in that time. Of course he wouldn't have lost himself immediately; the main cavern might still be within a few feet. He tried to imagine directions again and, with an effort, decided on the way back.

He walked smack into the wall almost immediately and had to concede that his sense of direction was thoroughly lost, along with himself. There was nothing more to do for the time being and he had the good sense to sit down and wait. The outlaws would return eventually and, unlike himself, they'd have the foresight to equip themselves with torches. He'd see the reflection of the flames. Unless he'd already wandered too far, his inner conscience added glee-fully, causing him to search through his clothes again, on the off chance a match still remained, hidden deep within a forgotten pocket.

It was a long shot that never paid off. There were no matches, and eventually he settled down again. It must be dark outside by now. Whoever was coming, they surely wouldn't return before morning, still several hours away by his reckoning. Somehow the thought of night outside made the cavern loom even darker than it was and the unseen drip of water even louder. Restlessly he threw off his stifling fears and tried to get some sleep.

It was the sound that awoke him. He didn't know whether he'd been asleep five minutes or five hours, but there was definitely someone moving about. Several people judging by the racket, though for the life of him he couldn't judge the direction. The clatter of booted feet seemed to echo from all points of the dark cavern. Fear began to crawl through his veins again, but he made a determined effort to thrust it to the back of his mind. He'd see the torches soon, very soon. He knew he would!

How long it was, he couldn't tell, but all of a sudden he realized the dancing shadows weren't a part of his own imaginings, but the result of a distant light source. It wasn't immediately obvious which direction he should follow, but when he edged cautiously towards his right and the shadows began to fade, he immediately turned around, striding out with renewed confidence.

Vaguely he was aware that men were talking, an excited chatter that refused to settle into any pattern he could understand. Suddenly, he gained the feeling of great space and relief flooded through him when he realized he must have entered the main chamber once more. As if to corroborate his feelings, at that moment a group of seven or eight men, most of them holding flaring torches, suddenly appeared in the mouth of a cave on his left flank. Having carefully noted the position of his exit, he sank into cover and watched their progress with interest.

The outlaw leader was in the van, with Sarah's cousin, Jamie, at his shoulder and the half-breed Indian, Santos, treading hard on their heels. The remainder of the crew, Johnny vaguely categorized as further members of the outlaw gang, some of whom he'd already seen.

'There.' Jamie pointed out the boxes excitedly and the outlaws surged forward, only to be held back by their leader, who began to issue orders.

'Open them up and check their contents,' he commanded peremptorily. 'Every last one of them.'

In order to create the maximum delay, Johnny had originally hoped the boxes would be transported outside before the gold was missed, but, in fact, the decision was to his immediate advantage. There was an initial cry of disappointment, swiftly followed by several others just as disheartening as each of the boxes was opened in turn. All attention was on the stone filled boxes, and the gunman took the opportunity to slip into the exit cave, where he followed the newly laid twine with little or no trouble until he reached the entrance. There, half way up the vent that led into the open, he heard the guards laughing at some unheard joke. Three, at least, he quickly estimated.

Damn it, I hadn't expected them to set a watch, the gunman castigated himself for his lack of forethought. They'd have got me too, he realized, if they'd been watching the cave. He began to think them negligent until he realized they were there to guard against someone approaching from the trail, not from within the cavern. Presumably they expected only friends to appear from that direction.

He allowed his right hand to touch his pistol momentarily before he made up his mind. There was no chance of rushing them, he decided, not when he had to negotiate a difficult entry before he could even think of opening hostilities.

He dropped back into the cave, then reluctantly headed towards the main chamber. The worst of all worlds would be to be caught between two parties; nor had he any desire to hide in a side passage having learned from bitter experience how easily he could become disoriented in the absolute darkness underground.

The party had broken up, torches flaring eerily from every corner of the cavern while the outlaws sought the missing gold bars. Johnny slipped into cover a little closer to them than before, too close he realized when he found the dark bulk of the outlaw chief looming no more than a few feet away. Jamie lay at his feet, and in the flaring light, Johnny could see the blood running down his face. Clearly he'd been held to blame for the whole affair.

'Santos. Over here.' The outlaw leader called out for his lieutenant in a commanding voice, and a moment later the dark, scarred face of the half-breed loomed out of the shadows.

'Make him talk.' He gestured carelessly at the prone figure by his feet, causing Jamie to draw up his legs with a whimper.

Santos didn't bother to answer, but all of a sudden

Jamie was hauled to his feet, bent awkwardly across a convenient boulder and threatened with a weaving flash of the Indian's knife.

'Tell us what happened.' The outlaw chief started the interrogation. 'Where's the gold?'

'It was here.' Jamie sounded very frightened, as well he might have been, his voice high with fear. 'It was here when we left.' His voice rose into a shriek when the half-breed growled and dropped the knife closer. 'Please, it was. We checked the boxes, we checked them all.'

'You took it. You and Nolan.'

'No, it wasn't me. I would never have led you here if I meant to keep the loot for myself.'

That was palpably true and the outlaw chief nodded in confirmation. Santos wasn't so trusting and his knife dipped, slicing open a cheek and frightening a howl of pain from the terrified lad.

'Stop. Let him talk.' The outlaw chief held up his hand, but his eyes still bored coldly into the unfortunate prisoner.

'It must have been Nolan.' Jamie was jabbering fearfully, his eyes glued to the slow waving of the Indian's knife hand, which seemed to be positioning itself for a foray at the other cheek. 'He told me we could keep it all if we kept the secret of the caves. If we killed the old man and that interfering fool of a cowboy, no one would even know there ever was a cave.' He whimpered. 'I told him I wouldn't do it.' His voice rose again in fright when the knife was laid against his skin. 'Told him we had to share. You're our friends.'

'Nolan.' The outlaw chief savoured the name for a moment as though he'd long held suspicions of the other's trustworthiness. 'Where is Randy? I don't remember seeing him on the trail.' He looked out over the figures still seeking for any clue to the gold's whereabouts.

'He's not with us.' Jamie was mesmerized by the Indian's blood-spattered blade that still threatened him. 'He rode off early this morning, returning to the ranch. Said he had a score to settle with my cousin. Said she'd looked down her nose at him once too often.'

Johnny ground his teeth helplessly. If he'd known that, he'd have risked the guards and fought it out at the entrance. Now he was trapped. He might have been able to worm his way back if it was just the outlaw chief close at hand, but Santos was all too alert, as he'd already found to his cost.

'He must have doubled back last night after we rode in to tell you where the gold was hidden. Nolan took it, not me.' Jamie was still passing the buck.

'It remains in the cave then,' decided the outlaw chief. 'Gold's heavy. He'd need a wagon, and there's no sign of tracks outside. Not that he'd have time to get one, or maybe that's why he rode down to the ranch this morning.' He laughed out loud, the harsh tones forming into an evil bray. 'He'll stay for the girl first. Randy is nothing if not predictable.'

'No, he'll be back,' prophesied Jamie desperately, his voice raised in fear of the Indian who held him captive. Santos was showing an impatience that boded ill for the man in his grip. 'He'll come back to collect the gold, he has to.'

'Very true,' the outlaw chief confirmed cheerfully. 'Finish him, Santos.'

The Indian's knife weaved over his captive, as though

searching for an opening, then bit, slicing easily through flesh and muscle. Jamie sagged, his dying scream bitten off with a fearful gurgle when his throat opened in a waterfall of blood.

'Take some men with you and bring Nolan back.' The outlaw's voice rang out harshly in a further command. 'Those lazy bastards watching the entrance will do, there's nothing here to guard for the time being. And make sure the dirty rat's alive, or I'll have you dancing to a tune you won't like. I'll keep the search up in here, but he must have all the answers.'

Santos nodded silently and strode off towards the exit.

Johnny watched while the outlaw went to rejoin his men, then silently followed in the half-breed's footsteps.

Climbing the final vent to the outside world was the worst moment. Perhaps a token guard had been left after all, perhaps Santos had somehow divined his presence. He hesitated, clinging on to the precarious hand-holds with his fingertips, listening carefully for several minutes before he finally burst out of hiding, gun in hand, ready to blaze away at anything that moved.

There was no one in sight and relief flooded through him as he began to breathe easier. The outlaws must have left their horses nearby – he'd steal one and follow Santos down to the ranch. He doubted whether the half-breed was going mob-handed just to capture Randy Nolan. The entire ranch, and all its occupants would be at his mercy, that is if Nolan hadn't already dealt out his own brand of death.

Horses there were, but two of the outlaws were guarding them, quite obviously alert to the possibility of ambush. Santos would have set the sentries himself in case he missed his quarry. If Nolan somehow eluded his Indian killer and was truly at fault, sooner or later he'd turn up to collect his gold, and a clutch of horses to act as pack beasts would present him with a golden opportunity. The gunman stared hungrily, planning his attack, patiently drawing up plans, only to discard them one by one. By making a beeline for the line hut he could have his own horse within the hour, whereas any attack on such a vigilant enemy must involve the use of guns. Santos would undoubtedly still be close enough to hear such a battle, and he had a bunch of outlaws to back him. Shots might even be heard underground and bring another pack of enemies boiling out of the cave behind.

He turned, and began to run towards the line hut, keeping up a punishing pace even when the blood began to boom in his head.

Johnny lay prone on a promontory above the hut and the tiny barn adjacent, watching carefully for any trace of habitation. He couldn't lay a finger on what troubled him, but neither did he intend to ignore his intuition. Something was different. Someone was there. Perhaps the outlaws had discovered the hut and set someone to guard over it.

Damn it, he couldn't wait any longer. Sarah was in danger, and so was everyone else at the ranch.

# CHAPTER TEN

# SARAH'S STORY

Despite his reservations Johnny realized he had to approach the hut with care. Whether he was already too late to save Sarah lay in the balance, but acting precipitately might result in his never arriving at the ranch to help her. He swore again silently, cursing the time his cautious approach was costing; cursing his decision ever to leave the horse; and cursing again when he realized that Santos would most surely have detected the animal had he hobbled it near the trail.

The hut itself had been built into an overhang of the rocky outcrop behind, and although it was beginning to show signs of wear and tear, had evidently been formed for easy defence, presumably against the Indian tribes that lived on the land before Sarah's grandfather. The barn which held his horse was of later construction, a simple, shingled roof built over a rift in the rocks, partially fenced in at the front, and only approachable over the open ground that fronted the shack. This had been cleared to present a direct field of fire some thirty yards out to the person defending the position. Or, as he had to ruefully admit, to anyone laying for a returning gunman.

Lying prone in the precarious cover afforded by a low, flat boulder that fronted the final approaches to the hut, Johnny scanned the narrow windows anxiously. There were two, flanking either side of the door which lay ever so slightly ajar. He couldn't see anyone watching, which, as he was well aware, meant nothing. He also knew he'd already exposed himself in reaching his present position. Maybe there was no one lying in ambush there! Or maybe they were patient enough to bide their time, waiting for a clear shot at a man, rather than loose off a round at a fleeting target.

He steeled himself and charged the door, his pistol ready to take any target that so much as shadowed the dingy glass in the window apertures. So far so good, he told himself when he threw his shoulder at the door. Already ajar, it gave easily, flinging itself back on its hinges, and reverberating with a shivering thud. He rolled desperately across the floor, his eyes questing the dim interior for any sign of an enemy gunman. A terrified scream erupted from the direction of the bed and he shifted his aim, only to find himself covering the cowering form of Sarah.

The surprise was complete and it took him a moment or two to take the picture in. She'd been sitting on the edge of the bed darning. Her tough work shirt by the looks of it, and badly torn too. He stared mesmerized; the garment lay on her lap and she wore only a camisole shift above her pants, cut low enough to show off the enticing curves of her bosom. The shift fastened down the front, and a couple of buttons at the top had torn loose, revealing a deep, rounded cleavage.

'Oh.' Sarah remained frozen for a moment or two

longer, then, when she saw where his eyes were resting, blushed rosily and covered herself with the ruined shirt. 'Johnny,' she faltered. 'I thought—'

Just what she might have thought remained unspoken. Throwing the shirt heedlessly to one side, the frightened girl flung herself headlong into his arms, twining her own around his neck and crushing her body against his own as if sheer physical contact could ease her own panic. He wound his free arm around her waist, and finding the pistol an unnecessary encumbrance, tossed it on to the bed, and began to gently stroke her hair while she wept gustily into his chest.

The scene changed in a second. Her sobbing calmed and she lifted her face to be kissed; then kissed him back, straining into him to prolong the caress. The kiss deepened and the blood began to pound through his veins. He gathered her closer, all too aware of how the soft weight of her breasts crushed against his chest and the thrust of her thighs against his own, were causing him to react. Her hips lunged, moving against his manhood with a wanton, unknowing shimmy, and he knew he had to act now or not at all.

Manfully thrusting down his rising libido, he grasped her shoulders firmly and held her at arms' length. There was a smoky glaze in her eyes, one he knew would be reflected in his own, and her lips were still open, shocked by the sudden removal of their contact. She shook her head and gasped.

'I—' Sarah seemed to realize just how exposed she was and turned away to grasp her shirt again. For a moment it seemed as though she would merely use the garment to cover herself, but then she turned back towards him and began to pull it on, making no attempt to hide her figure.

That simple act of dressing rapidly brought Johnny back to his senses, despite the flesh exposed to his gaze, and he began to consider their situation.

'What happened?' His first thoughts were of her. Why was she here? How the devil had she torn her clothes so badly?

Sarah took a moment longer to gather her scattered wits before she began to tell her story. 'Grandpa's dead,' she announced as a preamble, then broke down again, tears streaming down her face.

'How?' the gunman asked gently. He only had to look at her stricken expression to realize there was more to this than just the simple fact of her grandfather dying. She adored the old man, but he'd been fading fast and she'd already reconciled herself to his imminent death.

'It happened this morning.' Sarah forced back her tears with a gulp. 'I was taking Grandpa's medicine up to him before I started the chores. I went up the back stairs' – her grief made her explanation almost staccato – 'and I was almost at Grandpa's door before I saw him.' She paused, the full horror of the meeting in that dim corridor breaking in on her. 'It was Nolan,' she shivered miserably, her voice breaking under the strain of relating the sad tale. 'He was on his own, standing quietly in a gloomy alcove, leering at me. I asked him what the devil he was doing up there; told him he'd scared me out of my wits, but all he did was laugh.'

'I didn't pay him much attention at first, just put my nose in the air and attempted to walk around him, until he lounged out of shadows and made a grab at me.' Sarah shuddered at the distasteful memory. 'He caught hold of my arm, but I jerked it away and swung around him.'

' "Not this time, darling", he told me, and slipping an arm around my waist, leaned forward as if to kiss me.

'I slapped him. Hard! He'd tried it on before, but never gone that far. I made as if to walk off, but he grabbed my shirt, twisted it around his wrist and hauled me back, reeling me in like a fish on a line. That's when I realized he was in earnest and not just chancing his arm. I was too frightened to think clearly, only knew I had to get away. I lunged, flinging my whole weight into the effort and my shirt wrenched open. The echo of scattering buttons clinking on to the floor seemed to mesmerize him and I thought I'd made it, but he still had hold of one corner of the garment. It tore and I could feel his eyes on me.'

'By that time I was desperate enough to try anything. I dipped my shoulder and tried to slip out of the shirt, but he was too quick and the next moment he had me at close quarters again. I screamed, fighting and biting, my fists pummelling him, but he hardly seemed to notice. He was slobbering over my face and neck, and his dirty hands were all over me.'

Sarah was almost sobbing and Johnny began to grind his teeth in helpless anger.

'I was bent back,' she forced herself to continued, 'almost doubled over, and I knew I couldn't fend him off for much longer. Until Grandpa took a hand. God knows how he made it to his feet, let alone staggered across the room. He had a gun, but he dare not use it while my attacker had me held so close. Nolan didn't hesitate though. He reacted immediately, like he'd known the old man would be out to protect me. He drew and fired before either of us could react, then dived for the cover of an alcove a few yards down the corridor.'

'Grandpa was mortally wounded, even in my state of shock I could see that. He was still on his feet though, steadily firing at Nolan's position and commanding me to make my escape. "I'm an old man", he hollered, "due to die anyway. There's nothing you can do and I'd as soon die on my feet as in bed." '

Sarah sobbed out loud and Johnny gathered her into his arms again. 'I wasn't going to leave him to his fate,' she declared mulishly, 'but then he was hit again and went down. I flung myself over him. I don't know why. To protect him, I suppose. Even while I did it I knew he was dead; the back of his head had been blown off and there was no way he could have survived.'

The girl fell silent for a moment, her face deadly pale while she remembered the tragedy. 'That's when I heard Nolan. He was sniggering, thinking he was in command. But Grandpa had dropped his pistol when he fell and somehow it had ended up within inches of my face. I grabbed it and blazed away at the bastard. It was no use because he hunkered back into cover and I did him no damage. Nevertheless, for a moment or two, I was an avenging angel, and then the hollow click of an empty chamber brought me back to my senses.'

'No way was I going to let Grandpa's sacrifice be made in vain. I turned and ran, taking the back stairs three and four at a time. I suppose Nolan hesitated, making sure Grandpa was dead before he followed, because I was already at the door before I heard the echo of his boots on the stairs. He would have hesitated before he took that risk anyway. The back stairs are steep and narrow, and he'd have presented a pretty target if I'd been waiting for him with a loaded gun.'

'Not that I was going to waste time doing a fool thing like that! Instead I sprinted across the yard towards the cover provided by the out-houses out back and made it to the barn without detection. I collapsed against the big doors, gasping for breath and terrified Nolan would already be on my tail, but I didn't hear any more from him, not then. I dare say he was searching the house first. Slow work when a desperate woman might be lying in wait to ambush him.'

' "What the devil's going on?" Someone asked the question. I swung around and if the pistol hadn't already been emptied, Barney would have been in mortal danger. As soon as I realized who it was the sense of relief just flooded through me. I've never fainted in my life, but I was close to it then. My legs were like jelly, shaking and buckling at the knee, and then he was beside me, steadying me. "Grandpa's dead," I told him, "and Nolan's on the warpath."

' "Get your old mare," he told me, "and find Johnny. I'll deal with Nolan." ' Sarah's voice faltered. 'He looked so fierce, but Nolan's a killer and I couldn't leave Barney there at his mercy. Eventually we came to a compromise. Barney rode out to fetch the law up from town, and I came along to find you.'

'Will the sheriff come?' Johnny looked unconvinced. The ranch had already had trouble getting him to see to the rustlers.

'He'll have to this time,' declared Sarah. 'Grandpa's been murdered, and the sheriff won't be able to hide behind town boundaries on that score. Besides, even if he dared to let it ride, Judge Stone would soon overrule him. He's hated the very name of McKenzie since his daughter died, but he's still the voice of the law around here, and he takes that responsibility seriously.'

'Where's your horse?' The gunman felt a sudden qualm. He hadn't detected any sign of another animal. 'In the barn?'

'No.' Sarah's face clouded over again. 'Nolan came out of the house just as I set out. He managed to squeeze off a couple of shots and hit my mare. I didn't think anything of it at first, she galloped off bright as a button, and it was only later, on the trail, I realized it was serious. She finally gave out a mile or two back.'

'He didn't give chase?'

'No, my mare was already at the gallop when he saw me. By the time he'd saddled a horse and given chase I'd have been long gone. I took the back trail too; it's pretty rough and not easy to follow unless you know the country.'

That explanation satisfied the gunman. He'd begun to wonder just how she'd managed to escaped detection on the trail when it passed directly by the cave, and for some time he'd been darting sidelong glances towards the window in case the entire outlaw gang turned up to challenge them.

'What now?' Sarah had detected Johnny's worried demeanour, and, although the overwhelming relief of his presence wasn't about to evaporate, she began to realize they weren't out of the woods just yet.

The gunman didn't answer at once. There was too much to weigh up. Instead he asked a question. 'Did Barney get away?'

'Yes. He went off in the other direction. Didn't have to pass the house at all. Nolan may not even have realized he was there.'

'Was there anyone else on the ranch?'

Sarah shrugged her shoulders in blank denial. 'Our housekeeper is the only live-in staff we have left and she went into town yesterday to visit her sister with Mariella. I suggested they remain there for a few days until we had time to settle this business with the rustlers. I could look after Grandpa every bit as well as she.' The girl looked stricken when she mentioned her dead grandfather, but added a forlorn rider. 'I don't know about Jamie, he might still be there.'

'No, I've seen him already.' Johnny studied the options, weighing them in his mind. 'If we stay here,' he declared, 'there's a gang of outlaws a couple of miles down the trail that wouldn't hesitate to commit murder.' He considered the situation further and tempered his thoughts. 'On the other hand we're in a good position to defend ourselves so long as we can rely on the sheriff's posse arriving in good time to relieve us.'

'They will. Barney will make sure of that.'

Johnny wasn't so all-fired certain. He didn't want to dent the girl's new found confidence, but even though he'd known Barney for such a short time, he had no doubt the man would have turned back to the ranch the moment he heard Nolan open fire on the girl. He may yet have escaped the outlaw's pistol and made it into town, but that wasn't an absolute fact they could rely on.

'If we decided to leave,' he continued relentlessly, 'we could follow on my original plan and return to the ranch ourselves.' He considered the downsides. 'We know that Nolan's there and Sancho's been despatched to find him with maybe three or four others, but the posse would surely head that way first.' And we'd find out if Barney ever made it off the ranch, he concluded privately.

'Or we could pack up and head for town ourselves,' Sarah enunciated the final option for him.

Johnny felt strangely reluctant to take that course, though he recognized it was the safest for both him and the girl so long as they could clear the immediate neighbourhood. Perhaps it felt too much like running away, but if Barney hadn't made it into town, then at least he and Sarah could roust out the law. He strolled to the entrance and stood in the doorway to survey the surrounding countryside while he made his mind up.

A shot rang out, showering splinters from the wooden lintel over his head, and he reacted immediately, slamming the door shut with his left hand while his pistol sprang into his right. A flick of his wrist shattered the glass in one of the windows and, when a second shot thudded into the thick timbers of the door, he flattened himself against the wall beside it.

'Keep low,' he rapped out the command, 'and throw me that rifle.' Sarah had dropped into cover behind the bed, but the top of her head was still visible. He caught the weapon that she tossed across the room and thrust down his fears for her safety while he examined the rocky hillside. Another shot rang out and a portion of the wooden window frame erupted in a flurry of splinters. High on the hillside from the concealment of a jumble of rocks a faint puff of smoke momentarily appeared in the air, eddied, and was dissipated by the rising wind.

'Nolan,' the gunman announced grimly. 'It has to be Nolan.' He considered the other's situation. 'He didn't take after you at once because Barney was his primary target. He had to stop help being summoned at any cost.'

'How could he know Barney was there, let alone heading for town?' Sarah's face ran pale when the truth struck her. She began to whisper. 'The old fool went back to help me, didn't he? He heard the shots and turned around straight off.' She sobbed out loud. 'He's dead too.'

'Not necessarily,' Johnny tried to ease her pain. 'He

knows the ranch like the back of his hand. More likely he simply got pinned down. Nolan's only just arrived, or he'd have drilled me when I got here. Probably made off when Sanchos and his gang showed up at the ranch. They were under orders to take him back to face the music at the cave, but I suspect that's the last thing he wanted to do. Most likely he followed your trail, assumed you were alone, and got taken by surprise when I popped my head out. Let off a shot without thinking, or taking proper aim.'

'What now?' Johnny started when Sarah slid in close beside him and asked the question, the warmth of her body enveloping him like a comforting blanket.

'We stay here,' he told her with simple logic. The decision had been made the instant he knew Nolan was out there. The wide, open fire plain that made the cabin so defensible, also made it impossible to escape once an enemy had it under his guns. Barring a black, moonless night, they were at stalemate. The gunman slid a comforting arm around Sarah's shoulders and drew her close while the wind outside continued to rise. A black, moonless night was beginning to look like it was on the cards too, a storm was on the way.

Should he wait for help to turn up? Or go seek out his enemy? Simple reasoning suggested Barney hadn't escaped to warn the sheriff, so there was only one answer to that conundrum in the long run, but right then he didn't care to muse on it. Sarah was snuggled close in his arms and he dipped his head to kiss her. No more than a peck, a promise of more to come. Right at that moment he couldn't allow his attention to wander in case their enemy made a daring attempt to creep up on them.

119

# CHAPTER ELEVEN

# AN OLD FRIEND

Another shot. The sound echoed eerily around the hills and Johnny cautiously edged closer to the window embrasure, signalling Sarah to stay back. There'd been no sign of a shell striking the cabin and he wondered what new surprise Nolan had in store for them.

A sudden fusillade of gunfire opened up and he hit the floor, dragging the girl down with him. Time passed while he nestled under the window, his rifle at the ready, aware there was more than one gun in action. Had the other outlaws arrived to offer their help? No! An answer ready made when there was still no sign of the cabin being targeted. The sheriff's posse? Not likely. There wasn't the volume of gunfire to suggest a posse, though the shooting continued unabated and there was evidently a duel of some sort in progress. He eased himself into an upright position and peered cautiously from the relative safety provided by the thick window jamb. There was nobody in sight, but still the relentless explosion of rifle fire continued to echo around the valley.

Damn! It had to be Barney attempting a solo rescue and, with the outlaws close enough at hand to hear the battle, it could signal the end of them all. Trusting Nolan would have turned all his attention on the new arrival, the gunman threw caution to the winds, flung open the door and raced across the open ground to the relative safety of the rocky slopes in which Nolan had ensconced himself.

To Johnny's relief the surprise was complete. Nolan failed to fire a single shot at him while he sprinted for cover. Indeed he may not even have realized the gunman was on the loose until he opened up, his fire covering a manoeuvre from their unknown supporter, briefly silhouetted against the skyline when he advanced. Too tall and slim for Barney Tolittle. Who the devil was it?

Johnny had no time available to ponder on an answer to that question. As soon as Nolan realized he was facing an enemy on two fronts, he switched his fire to the gunman's more exposed position. Johnny squeezed deeper into the precarious cover of a boulder, wincing when shells ricocheted off the stone with a high-pitched whine, splattering tiny fragments all around.

A brief cessation occurred while Nolan fired on their unknown ally in an attempt to delay his advance and Johnny took his chance. Deeper cover was only a jump away and he flung himself at it, a near thing when Nolan switched his aim back on the gunman, taking a chunk of rock off his new cover. One razor sharp shard sliced open his forehead and for a moment he thought he'd been hit. Then, wiping himself with the back of his hand to clear the fresh blood from his eyes, he wriggled towards a natural embrasure and snapped off a few shots of his own.

Nolan gave up. Caught between two adversaries he chose the path of least resistance. The rocky background offered an easy path to retreat in safety and the echo of his horse's hoofs marked the end of any attempt to hunt him down. Cautiously Johnny stepped out into the open, to be joined a moment later by the tall, emaciated figure of Pieter Rorovitz.

Having thanked Pieter for his timely intervention, the three of them settled down in the snug interior of the cabin to discuss their next move.

'How did you get here, Pieter? I thought you weren't intending to involve yourself in anything that wasn't your fight.'

'It became my fight.' Bitterness had added an even more guttural edge to Pieter's accent. 'I managed to sell my farm in town, not a big sum, not when those thieving bastards at the bank could smell a bargain. Nevertheless it was enough for Mariella and me to move on and next morning I set off to pick her up. She'd run away, of course. Damned fool idea to board her with Mrs Pugh. She probably wanted to send the girl to school or sit around all lady-like in a pretty dress with bows and furbelows all over it. Damn, but it never did do no good to try and hedge Mariella around, and so I told the interfering old bag. No matter; I knew she'd run off to the ranch and I was content to pick her up on the trail.'

Pieter's exasperation showed through. 'I don't know how she made it in the time, stole a horse I reckon, but I didn't come on her until I was almost at the McKenzie ranch. It was still early and she was sneaking around the barns, keeping under cover. I wondered about her behaviour at the time, but didn't subscribe any particular reason to it. Guess she must have known something was up.'

'Nolan and my grandpa fought,' Sarah supplied the missing details. 'She may have heard the gunfire.'

'Next thing I knew,' Pieter continued without acknowledging the interruption, 'Miss Sarah was galloping out as if the devil was on her heels and there was Nolan, himself, blazing away at her with his pistol. Damned fool trick, she was way too far out for him to hit her with that little pop gun.'

'He hit my horse though.' Sarah interrupted him again to make the comment.

'I saw the mare lying dead on the back trail,' agreed Pieter. 'Anyhow, you was off and safe, but Mariella had gone to ground, so I dismounted and began to scout around out back. Nolan was still standing in the front yard, evidently deciding what to do next, when Barney Tolittle suddenly steamed in. I suppose he already knew what to expect because he blasted away with that old shotgun of his without any hesitation. I made sure Nolan was a goner, but I guess it ain't so easy to fire straight from the back of a horse and the twisted little devil somehow managed to dive into cover and open up himself.

'Hit Barney too. The old fool toppled off his horse, but he wasn't so bad hurt he couldn't run. Fired the second barrel on the hoof and scared Nolan so hard he retreated back on to the porch and took cover behind the old water butt. Next thing I knew Barney had Mariella under his arm and was diving into the shelter of that old water trough out front of the house.

'It was a stand-off. Neither of them had what you'd call good cover, but neither of them could shift either. Not

when they were under each other's guns. I guess I was the
ace in the hole, but I couldn't reach Barney and Mariella
where they were, nor dare alert Nolan to my presence by
calling them. Instead I started to work myself around the
outbuildings, well out of sight, flitting carefully from barn
to barn, aiming to enter the house from the rear and
surprise Nolan that way.

'I nearly did it too. I was actually inside the house when
another bunch of outlaws turned up and took matters into
their own hands. It was the sudden fury in the shooting
that alerted me. There wasn't much point to Nolan and
Barney exchanging shots like that, so I soon judged someone else was on the scene, just didn't know who it could
be.

'I scooted up the back stairs and ran straight into the
colonel's body. It was like a slaughter house in the top hall,
blood spattered everywhere. Nolan's work, I guess, but I
didn't have time to ponder on it. I made my way around to
the front, a lady's bedroom from the look of it. Nice set of
drapes to hide behind while I spied out the lie of the land.

'I recognized most of them, half a dozen at least, with
that devil-spawned half-breed, Santos, in the lead. They
had Barney and Mariella held up at gun-point. The old
man was lying on the floor and it looked like he'd been
wounded again, because Mariella was trying to bind his leg
with some sort of rag while they all looked on. No sign of
Nolan like I expected; reckon he knew when he wasn't
wanted, or perhaps that he was. Anyhow Santos roared out
his orders. The house was to be searched and Nolan taken
alive.

'That got me running scared. Nolan must have slipped
into the house, no other way for him to go. Knowing they

were after him, he'd be madder than a cornered rattler and in no mood to pick his target before he blazed away. And if he didn't get me, there were half a dozen outlaws scouring the place that would. It was a poor choice, but I had to attempt an escape and trust to luck I didn't run into anyone on the way.

'Somehow it weren't that much trouble. Nolan obviously knew the layout of the house, and I dare say he was out through the kitchen before the outlaws even braved the front door. I wasn't far behind because I saw the dust kicked up by his horse, heading for the back trail, same as you, Miss Sarah. I'd been terrified I'd be trapped upstairs, but the outlaws were playing safety first and advancing with care. Guess I'd have done the same if I thought a gunman like Nolan might be laying for me around the next corner.

'There were another couple of the varmints heading for the barns, but I had my horse staked way off, up by that stand of old cottonwood.' Johnny calculated the distance and nodded. Pieter was nothing if not careful, that particular copse had to be half a mile back from the ranch proper.

'I stuck around a time to see what happened, but I couldn't fight a whole bunch of outlaws on my own and, since it looked as though they intended to hold Barney and Mariella prisoner rather than harm them, I judged it best to join forces with Miss Sarah. I guessed she was going for help, and since the area around the ranch was becoming a mite unfriendly, I decided to follow her trail.'

Pieter paused a moment. 'It didn't occur to me that Nolan was following her as well, not until I heard the shooting up ahead.'

'Where were Barney and Mariella when you last saw them?' Johnny put the question to Pieter.

'They were herded up on the porch where Barney was trussed up to one of the supports. He had some sort of tourniquet wrapped around his leg, but it didn't look as though it was troubling him much. Mariella was sat in an old rocking chair, tied down by the looks of it, but otherwise none the worst for wear. Santos had detailed one of the men to watch them and there were a couple more patrolling the perimeter. I reckon they'd already realized Nolan was long gone, because the rest of them were set out to work in one of the barns. Sounded to me like they were hitching up the horses to one of the heavy wagons.'

'They need a wagon to transport the gold,' declared Johnny. 'If they ever find it! What about Santos?' The Indian would be their most difficult foe should they have to mount a rescue.

'He lit out on his own. Back up the trail towards the bluffs.'

'Gone to report back to his boss, no doubt.' Johnny made his decision. 'Sarah, you take my horse and head off into town to fetch the sheriff. Pieter and I will have to ride double down to the ranch to see what we can do to help. Barney and Mariella seem safe enough for the present. Trussed up as they are they can't harm the gang, but a band like this is capable of anything.'

'You'll kill that horse under the weight of the pair of you.' The girl stared disdainfully at Pieter's scraggy mount, then continued heatedly. 'In any case, I'm going to the ranch with you.'

Johnny looked like he was going to argue the point, but desisted when he saw the determined thrust of her chin and the flashing light of battle in her eyes.

'I can hop up on the pommel before you,' she told the gunman in measured tones. 'There's no sense in splitting our forces, but if you're determined to fetch the sheriff right away, send Pieter.'

'I'd have to be a fool to do that,' declared Pieter stridently, then surprised them both with a bald confession. 'The sheriff's in this whole damn business up to his neck and my life won't be worth a cent if he gets hold of me.' He paused and nodded significantly in Sarah's direction. 'Nor will anyone else's if he thinks I've told on him.'

'The sheriff?' Sarah exclaimed in surprise. 'Grandpa always said he was nothing but a damned carpet-bagger, but this beats everything. Are you sure of what you're saying?'

'He's their leader, the one that had me kidnapped. I dare say he was in it with James when they robbed the bank in the first place. There had to be an inside man, and he was a trusted deputy back then. The rustlers had never been more than a nuisance before, but when the colonel got sick, the sheriff must have seen his chance and taken charge. No doubt he always suspected the old man of hiding his son, but the colonel's a tough man to face down, even from his sickbed, and the sheriff couldn't risk searching the place in his official capacity. There'd be too many witnesses and he wanted to keep the gold for himself.'

'So he turned up the heat on the rustlers and started to pick off the hands one by one?' Johnny supplied the sheriff's strategy.

'Sure thing. I dare say their plan was to walk in as soon as the old man died. He was a tough old bird who was well

127

respected in the neighbourhood. Guess they couldn't just go in and shoot him down without raising the sort of ruckus that might preclude a thorough search of the place. If the gold was hidden there it could take them weeks to find.'

'Taking the place from his granddaughter might have raised a ruckus too,' Johnny observed.

'Not if they had young Jamie waiting in the wings,' declared Pieter. 'The colonel's only grandson, and son of his eldest son to boot. There's many a judge would back his claims legally, and with him nominally in charge, even if it were only temporary, the search could proceed with impunity.'

'If he thought the gold was hidden on the ranch, why kidnap you?' Johnny interrupted again.

'Young Jamie was sent in with Nolan to spy. They soon uncovered evidence of my part in James's escape and questioned me. I didn't know where the gold was hidden, but no one gives a damn about me, so they were free to take me and use more persuasive measures. That's when I first discovered the sheriff was in with them. He led the questioning and it soon became obvious he was their leader. Despite his beatings I had nothing to add to what he already knew and, believe me, being so scared for my life I'd have told them anything. I think he already knew that, but he still turned me over to Santos for further interrogation. That half-breed's the very devil in disguise and I could only thank God he'd not been brought in before. I played sick, easy to do when you've taken the sort of beatings they hand out. Then, when they relaxed their guard, I managed to escape, barely a hop and a skip in front of the Indian.'

'There're other people in town. The judge—'

'Everyone in town believes I'm nothing but a waster,' Pieter broke in at once. 'No one would take me seriously. You could all be dead before I managed to raise a posse. Besides, Miss Sarah's right about our forces. No necessity to split us up just yet. You may need another gun down at the ranch if that gang of desperadoes is still in occupation there.'

Johnny shrugged his shoulders in a dismissive gesture. 'It won't come down to a gunfight,' he declared. 'We can't mount an attack while Barney and Mariella are still captive. Our best hope of rescuing them is to wait until most of the gang have returned to the caves with the wagon.'

# CHAPTER TWELVE

## BACK AT THE RANCH

They took the back trail on their journey towards the ranch. Sarah had hopped up on to the pommel in front of Johnny, cosily ensconcing herself in the crook of his arm, and Pieter, divining their desire to be alone together, had elected to ride a length or two in advance.

'Why are you doing this for us, Johnny? Pieter and I have lives and property at stake, but you could up and go if you wanted to. You'd be a whole lot safer if you just cut and run.'

The gunman already knew his answer, had done ever since he'd spoken to her grandfather, but he wanted more time to woo the girl. Time he didn't have! This was neither the time nor the place to act like a lover, but, however reluctantly, he decided to declare himself.

'I have a stake too,' he told her tenderly. 'You're the woman I want to spend the rest of my life with, if you'll have me.'

house they could see the dark clouds building, an ebony mass inexorably bearing down on them.

'There'll be a storm soon enough,' Pieter prophesied while they crept forward to survey the situation at closer hand. And, as if to corroborate his words, a rumble of thunder sounded far off.

'True enough.' Johnny spoke absently, his eyes remaining on the still figures that decorated the veranda out front of the main house. 'Barney's able to move at least,' he declared at last, a whistled hiss of air from his lungs signalling his satisfaction when a slight shift of stance showed the loyal old hand was still alive. For long minutes they'd kept the two prisoners under surveillance, half afraid they'd been murdered in their bonds. 'Anyone spot any sign of the outlaws? There's bound to be a guard, unless they've abandoned the place altogether.'

'No.' Pieter whispered the denial, 'but they may be busy inside, ransacking the place.'

'Go search the barns, Pieter,' the gunman replied, knowing his companions instinctively looked for him to take the lead, 'and I'll take the bunk house.' He pointed out the most exposed of the buildings. 'Sarah, you'll swing out left far enough to check out the backyard.' He stared at both of them seriously. 'Don't show yourself, and whatever happens, don't open fire unless your life is in danger. We'll regroup back here as soon as possible.'

It took the gunman very little time to check the bunkhouse was empty and return, and a moment later Sarah slipped silently into place beside him.

'Nothing to see out back,' she informed him quietly.

Pieter was longer in the coming, and Johnny was beginning to think he'd run into trouble when he finally arrived, still breathless from the final sprint over the open ground towards their cover.

'The heavy wagon's missing,' he told them. 'Guess the entire gang might have gone with it.'

'Maybe.' Johnny surveyed the buildings again. If guards had been left then they were waiting inside the house. Knowing the sort of man he had to contend with, it would be no surprise to find they were ransacking it, but he couldn't rule out another option. Perhaps they were covering the approaches from the windows, might even be watching them covertly at this very moment. He raked each of the visible windows with a steely stare, but was forced to admit he could see nothing out of place. It meant nothing, as he well knew from his own past experience. If a gunman was lying in wait for them, he'd take good care to remain unseen.

'Cover me if needs be,' he decided at last, and set off before either of his companions could object.

His immediate object was the bunkhouse. It was the closest structure to the near side of the house and the veranda on which the prisoners were confined. He could also gain its cover without revealing himself to anyone in the ranch house. From there he'd have to rely on surprise and the sheer speed of his sprint to the veranda. He grinned, all at once realizing what a fool he'd look if no guard had been left on the prisoners, an amusement that was as suddenly extinguished. There was someone there! Had to be, or Barney would have been working on his bonds.

His flesh crawled and his legs began to shake when he made his move, but his fear vanished under the sudden surge of adrenalin, so much so that he barely registered

Barney's reaction. He wasn't even aware that his erstwhile companion had realized help was at hand until the elderly cowboy kicked up his legs and stove in the window immediately to his right. That action, aside from very probably saving his life, gave the gunman a target.

He fired on the run, cleared the railings around the veranda in a single bound, fired again and dived through the remains of the window embrasure, his pistol still pumping out lead. It was the only way to ensure the two captive prisoners on the veranda didn't come under fire, but pure foolishness, as he realized. Nevertheless, the very audaciousness of the move had transfixed the enemy and he landed safely inside the room, rolling and twisting to throw off their aim while he attempted to draw a bead on the first man to come into his sights.

The outlaw was backing swiftly out of the room, but still trying to track Johnny's manoeuvres with his rifle. Pistol and rifle both fired in the same instant, each with as little success. The gunman's constant movement confused his own aim as much as the outlaw's, and a moment later the man had disappeared through the open doorway, slamming the door behind him.

Johnny's gun swung around to cover the remaining outlaw. He was sprawled out on the floor, his rifle thrown several feet away and his head a blinded mask of blood from the glass shards that had apparently exploded in to his face. Whether Barney's first kick had done the damage or it was due to his own entry through the remnants of the window, Johnny neither knew nor cared. The man had raised his hands in surrender and the gunman urged him to join the others on the veranda with a careless gesture of his pistol.

He followed on, carefully slipping a pistol out of the other's belt, before surveying the scene. Barney was struggling in his bonds, cursing and swearing, while Pieter and Sarah were racing across open ground towards them. Johnny ruthlessly slammed the barrel of his pistol down on the back of the outlaw's head and drew his knife to slice open the knots that held Barney captive, leaving the old-timer free to deal with Mariella, who was quietly sobbing on the ancient rocker. There was a sudden clatter of hoofs from behind the house, heralding the departure of the other outlaw, and Johnny leapt off the veranda to draw a bead on his retreating form. His pistol spat fire again and again, but without any visible result until he realized the man was already out of effective pistol shot. Swearing crudely under his breath, Johnny reholstered his gun and made his way back to his companions.

Pieter and Sarah had arrived by this time, and while the one comforted his daughter, the other busied herself on checking out Barney's bloodied leg. Despite Pieter's assertion that he'd been hit a second time, there was only one wound and the old hand made his feelings known in no uncertain way.

'Stop flustering around me, woman,' he complained, 'it's nothing but a scratch.' However, for all the crusty old foreman's outward testiness, Johnny suspected Barney was secretly rather pleased at all the attention Sarah was lavishing on him.

A low groan brought the gunman's mind back to the job in hand. The outlaw was lying prone where he'd dropped, but already beginning to regain consciousness. Johnny grabbed his shirt front and hauled him off the floor.

'Start talking,' he hissed, and waved his pistol in front of the man's lolling head, aiming to catch the man unawares while he was still half conscious.

'What—' The outlaw opened his eyes and stared, mesmerized by the slow waving of the pistol in front of his eyes.

'Where's your friend gone? Where'd the rest go?' Johnny started the questioning in clipped accents.

'The cave.' The outlaw's voice was weak, but quite audible to the gunman.

'And the rest?'

'They took the wagon a couple of hours since.' He started when Johnny cocked the pistol. 'Please no,' he whined. 'They took it up to the caves, up there on the bluffs. It's too big to get off the trail. You're bound to see it if you go that way.' The man issued a staccato confession in his fear.

'What about the gold?' Johnny's questioning was ruthless, his eyes boring into the frightened outlaw.

'Santos will have found it by now. He's the very devil at tracking, better than any full-blood Indian I ever saw. They reckon Randy hid it for himself, damn his eyes. Most probably they'll be loading up by now. Please, I'm telling you the truth. Don't kill me.'

With a final oath, Johnny flung the outlaw back on to the floor. 'Stay there,' he ordered, 'and don't move a muscle.'

'Barney,' he turned to his companions and spoke after a moment's thought. 'Are you well enough to ride into town and raise a posse?'

'Sure thing, Johnny,' the old timer replied. 'I can sit a horse, no trouble, but if I hitch up the buckboard, I can

137

take Sarah in too.'

Johnny had already considered that option, but privately he considered Sarah was safer remaining on the ranch. One of the outlaws had returned to the band, no doubt bringing news of the captives' release. The sheriff, if he were truly their leader, would more than likely believe the rescue had been effected by a posse called out from town and, if anything, make ready to ambush them, unless he was already in a position to load up the wagon, in which case he'd cut and run as soon as he could. Either way he was unlikely to mount an attack on the ranch. There was, however, a chance he'd call the situation right and attempt to cut them off from town.

'Sarah can stay here,' he decided. 'Pieter and Mariella too. I need someone on the ranch to guard our prisoner. He knows too much about us to risk his escape. Besides, you'll make it into town on a horse before the outlaws have the chance to cut your trail, no such guarantee if you travel by buckboard. Don't talk to the sheriff, he's thrown his lot in with the outlaws. Not that he'll be in town; if I'm any judge he'll still be deep in the caves searching for that gold. I'll take a ride over there to see how they're getting on.'

'I can go with you just so long as we don't go underground.' Pieter made the offer, but added a hangdog rider. 'I never could stomach that stifling darkness, not like James. He was always exploring one cave or another.'

Johnny could see the cowboy's heart wasn't in it, even without the added complication of the caverns. 'No, thanks Pieter,' he replied. A companion on such a desperate enterprise would have been welcome, but he knew it was none of the other's business. 'If it comes to a fight I'd

138

rather be alone, when I can shoot at anything that moves.' The speech was a small sop to Pieter's conscience, but one that relieved the erstwhile ranch-hand. Pieter didn't care whether or not the bank retrieved its gold, and neither should he.

Damn it. Johnny knew his own thoughts, knew he did care, and asked the question of himself. Why the hell should I? He couldn't have explained his feelings in words, but deep inside he knew it would in some way help to redress the wounds of his own desperate past. He'd do it for Sarah, for his parents, for himself. Though none but he would ever know to what lengths he was prepared to go to return the property of a bank he'd never seen, for the people of a town he'd never even visited.

'I'm coming with you.' Sarah's expression had taken on a mulish stubbornness that died stillborn under the gunman's anger.

'No!' Johnny rapped out the word. 'Not this time, Sarah.' He paused and softened his tone. 'I'm not going to put myself in any danger. Not unless they look like getting clear away, and there's precious little chance of that.'

'Johnny.' There was an anguished look on her face that made the gunman's heart flip. For a moment it looked as though she'd argue, but she suddenly turned away, tears starting in her eyes.

'All right, I'll stay,' she finally agreed, forcing the words regretfully through faltering lips.

# CHAPTER THIRTEEN

# IN AT THE DEATH

Johnny rode back to the cavern using the same back trail they'd already traversed. Despite his fears that the gang might already be making a swift getaway, he travelled at a leisurely pace, conserving his mount and trying to outguess his opponents. What would he do in their circumstances?

One of the outlaws they'd attacked had made his escape from the ranch, presumably fleeing back to the main party to bring word that the captives had been rescued. Did the outlaw know how many of them were in the party that attacked him? Johnny assumed not; he wouldn't have had the leisure to count them accurately. On the other hand their approach must have been spotted for an ambush to be staged in the first place. That being so, the outlaws must have realized they were facing a relatively small party. Whether he and his companions had been recognized or not was another matter. On the whole Johnny thought not; they'd presumably been

140

detected too far off for accurate identification and the action had passed too fast for coherent thought. They may well have been mistaken for an advance party of the inevitable posse, an event the outlaw's leader must surely be hourly expecting since he knew Sarah was still at large.

They'd divide the gang, he decided at last. Even if the town hadn't yet been alerted, it would be rash in the extreme to assume the freed hostages wouldn't raise the alarm. The main trail up to the caverns from the ranch ran through several narrow defiles on its way up to the bluffs, any one of which could easily be held by a bunch of determined men. Unless they'd already cleared the gold, holding up the posse must be their first priority when Johnny had deliberately dropped the gold into water deep enough to make it difficult to raise, all of which would necessarily delay their escape.

There'd be other men above ground too. The remuda, as he already knew, had been established off the trail near the cave. One or two men at most would be on guard, probably set to guard the wagon too. The remainder would be needed underground to recover the gold. Mentally Johnny deployed the outlaws, satisfied with his logic. He had only to pick off the guard on the horses and he was home and dry. One man with a gun could hold the entrance to the cavern for ever.

The first spots of rain began to fall when he reached the line hut, but he gave them no thought and, after tethering his horse in the old barn behind, pushed on towards the cavern on foot. Lightning was flashing in the distance and the rumble of thunder reached his ears, causing him to curse himself for leaving his slicker in his pack. The rain wasn't yet heavy, nor even constant, but a storm was all too evidently brewing and holding the entrance would be an uncomfortable business without shelter.

His first inkling that everything wasn't going his way came when he edged into the jumble of rocks about the cavern's entrance. He'd deliberately taken up his position on a prominent outcrop with a wide view over the surrounding countryside and the outlaws' horses and their guards should have been clearly visible. They weren't, and had all too evidently been moved. How far? The gang would need those horses handy to make their escape and they wouldn't be so far removed that the guards were out of earshot. If he had to open fire, he'd very soon find them closing in on his hiding place. Or had the outlaw gang already recovered the gold and left?

No! He carefully shifted his position to overlook the trail more easily. It was almost directly beneath him and now he could clearly see the heavy wagon they'd taken from the ranch, anxiously guarded by four heavily armed men. Partially loaded too, judging from the uneven humps plainly visible under the cover of the thick tarpaulin. With such a strong guard set, Johnny knew the outlaws must have discovered where he'd hidden the gold. Only a small portion of the hoard had been recovered so far, but no doubt the remainder of the outlaw gang would be deep underground busily recovering the remaining bars.

He slipped carefully through a maze of rock towards the entrance of the cave, realizing his plans were in tatters. Any attempt he made to hold the entrance to the cave would be thwarted by those guarding the wagon, let alone any further guards on the horses. If he should alert them by opening up himself he'd quickly be forced to retreat in the wake of their murderous crossfire. With that thought in mind he slithered through the rocks into a position where he could watch both the wagon and the general area of the cave's entrance.

Plan after plan ran through his brain only to be ruthlessly rejected when its shortcomings became apparent. The truth was plain to see; while the enemy had him outnumbered above ground, there was nothing he could do to delay their recovering the gold. He began to survey the cliffs up above, flinching against the heavy droplets of rain which were beginning to fall with ever increasing frequency. If he could find a secure position that overlooked the cavern and also provided him a sufficient wide field of fire to hold back the guards outside, perhaps he could still delay the outlaw's escape.

That was when he caught a glimpse of someone's shadow. At first he thought it was another of the outlaw band skulking through the rocks, perhaps even stalking him. He slipped though an angle of the rocks that took him out of sight for a moment and clambered higher, seeking the chance to neutralize at least one of his enemies. The figure reappeared lower down the slope and a moment later he pounced, only recognizing her at the moment of impact. They went down together in a heap and he swiftly covered her mouth to cut off her cry of alarm.

'Damn you, Sarah,' he hissed angrily. 'I thought you were staying on the ranch. I could have killed you.'

'You almost did,' the girl replied with remarkable coolness considering the shock her system had suffered. She brushed off the hand shielding her face and rubbed her behind ruefully. 'How come I end up breaking your fall?'

'Quiet! They're all around us.' Johnny hissed, laying a

warning finger over her lips, and, well aware of the racket they'd made in the brief scuffle, he strained his every sense towards the nearest of their enemies. He sighed in relief; no one seemed to have noticed. 'What the devil are you doing here?'

'I told you I was coming with you.'

'And I thought we'd agreed you weren't.'

'You agreed,' she answered sweetly. 'Not me.' Then quite unnecessarily she continued to explain her presence. 'I followed you as far as the line hut, but you quite outpaced me on foot.'

The storm broke with a violence that utterly overwhelmed them. The sunlight that had been failing steadily for some time under a potent threat from the rapidly encroaching ebony clouds, suddenly faded completely when the heavens opened in a steady downpour. The thunderous roar of falling water was echoed by the continuous peels of thunder that reverberated around the cliffs and Johnny drew the girl forward towards the cavern's entrance.

A blinding flash and the gunman suddenly realized they weren't alone. The entrance to the cave was at their feet and a guard had been mounted at its very lip. Sarah shrieked out loud, the sound plucked from her mouth by the wind, and a moment later Johnny had her in his arms, disappearing down the yawning gap at their feet. The guard had made no attempt to stop them, perhaps hadn't even seen them so momentarily had they been illuminated by the lightning.

Once they'd slipped into the passage the roar became muted, muffled as though heard from a distance and they were able to take stock of their situation. Both were soaked through to the skin, but that wasn't Johnny's primary concern.

'Keep close,' he commanded, taking Sarah's hand firmly in his own. 'We can't afford to be caught in this passageway.' His other hand sought out the guide rope and he began to walk at a steady pace despite the pitch black. Far in the distance he'd spotted a flickering echo of the outlaw's torches.

Hidden in the lee of a boulder close to the passage that led up to the entrance, Johnny and Sarah stared out on a scene of industry under the flare of a dozen or more torches. Several of the men were out on the water, operating from a hastily constructed raft, diving to set the heavy gold bars into wickerwork baskets which were then hauled out on to the raft for eventual transfer to dry land. A large pile lay at the feet of the outlaw leader who was directing operations.

'That's the sheriff,' whispered Sarah. 'I never did take to him, and neither did Grandpa.'

Johnny ignored her comment. 'They must have recovered most of the hoard by now,' he declared. 'Time to make our presence known.' He felt a sudden qualm in placing Sarah in danger, but couldn't think of anything else to do. If he did nothing, they'd have to move away from the exit and allow the outlaws to escape. He knew from bitter experience that once the torches had been extinguished and the pitch darkness allowed to return, both he and the girl would be in even greater danger, facing the prospect of losing their way in a maze of caverns. Completely sure in his mind he was in the right, he drew his pistol and fired.

145

The results were almost comical. He hadn't drawn a bead on anyone, seeking only to draw attention to the fact their escape was cut off, but the shot echoed off the walls and ceiling, amplified and reverberated as though a dozen men had opened fire, and in that moment pandemonium reigned. Everyone in sight attempted to duck into cover however inadequate, while those out on the water flung themselves flat on the flimsily constructed decking. The raft, not designed for such rapid manoeuvres, immediately overturned, throwing men and gold alike into the water, amid a frenzied welter of screaming and cursing.

Several of the men took out their pistols and fired back, though they had no real target in mind, such was the echo from every corner of the cave; it was a mind-blowing maelstrom of fire only amplified by their own shooting.

'Cease fire!' The sheriff shrieked out his command, but it was several minutes before he could make his authority felt.

'Who's there?' he continued at last.

Johnny diplomatically maintained his silence, but the outlaw leader wasn't to be gainsaid. If he couldn't see his assailants, at the very least he had the wit to recognize they'd barricade the entrance.

'Tom,' he called. 'Take a couple of the men and close in from the right.' He himself shifted the opposite way, calling forward another bunch of the outlaw gang, but the gunman had no intention of allowing himself to be outflanked.

'Keep their heads down,' he urged Sarah. 'A couple of shots should suffice, the echo will do the rest.' Both Sarah and he opened fire at the same moment, neither attempting a kill; they only needed to bottle up their enemies until the expected posse appeared. Two or three shots was all that was necessary. The resulting cacophony as the fire echoed back from wall and ceiling, added to by an enthusiastic response from some of the gang members, was enough to send everyone scurrying for cover once more.

The echoes died, but the sheriff remained silent for long minutes until Johnny began to wonder if he'd been killed, or at least injured, in the short burst of gunfire. A sibilant echo of whispering amongst the men deep in the cavern, however, soon convinced him their leader was still alive and kicking. Orders were evidently being passed, this time in a much more circumspect manner, and the first concrete response evident to the pair blockading the entrance came in the form of extinguishing several of the torches.

Johnny had no problem with this. Those torches that remained still provided a background light which would silhouette any outlaw rash enough to try and rush their position. In any case, judging from the inaccuracy of the returned fire, most, if not all of the outlaws, were unaware of exactly where he and Sarah were hidden. A further signal saw all but one of the remaining torches flicker and die, and Johnny smiled grimly, lack of light would provide no problems for them so long as he and Sarah remained together. It was inconceivable that the outlaws could close in on them in the dark without raising some sort of disturbance, and while they could fire at the slightest rustle in complete safety, their attackers would have to distinguish between friend and foe before shooting.

Long minutes passed in utter silence and Sarah backed up to him, seeking solace from his touch in the still darkness, which was almost complete in the far reaches around the entrance. He reached out one hand and squeezed her shoulder to reassure her.

'What are they doing?' she whispered hoarsely.

'No idea,' he returned in low undertones, 'but I expect they'll try to rush us sooner or later.'

In fact Johnny himself was rather puzzled by the extended silence. If the outlaws were intending to mount a direct frontal assault on their position, then it were best done immediately, rather than let shredded nerves get the better of them. Or perhaps the renegade sheriff had already ordered an attack, and the men had mutinied. He eased himself higher, trying to piece together any clues that might be offered. The silence continued and no one appeared to be on the move.

'Looks to me like they're going to sit it out,' he informed Sarah quietly, still wondering at this inexplicable decision on the part of their enemies. They must be aware a posse would be formed eventually, and once it arrived their criminal careers would be over.

At length a rising murmur from their enemies seemed to signal the next stage of their siege. The gunman extended his gun arm and prepared to pick off anyone unwise enough to expose himself in the flicker of the remaining torch. A shadow moved, far down by the water and the murmuring began to extend. More and more of the further off shadows began to move and all of a sudden the single remaining torch was extinguished.

Johnny felt Sarah's muscles tense when she brought her rifle up to her shoulder and immediately began to warn her.

'No,' he whispered. 'That flame went out by itself. The water's rising. Had to, I suppose. The storm's probably still raging outside.' He considered their own position in relation to the rising waters with some satisfaction. The entrance they guarded lay at one of the highest points in the central cavern which sloped down towards the water, and so far as he knew it was the only way out. The outlaws would have to surrender or risk everything in an all-out attack, and judging from the rapidly increasing roar that marked the surging waters, that decision would have to be made soon.

The eerie, ear-splitting howl startled Johnny as much as anyone, but he immediately perceived his own folly in believing that none of the outlaws could approach in complete silence. The brawny figure of the Indian half-breed, Santos, followed the war cry out of the darkness immediately and the gunman barely had time to react. That his belly wasn't opened at the outset by the slashing knife was due as much to Santos's mistimed leap as his own desperate manoeuvres, the only sign Johnny had so far seen that the Indian was as blinded by the complete darkness as he himself.

He closed immediately, sensing the powerful half-breed would have no compunction in disabling Sarah, who'd opened fire again in reply to a crescendo of shots echoing from the outlaws' position. Somehow, the echoing shots seemed dulled by the increasing roar of flood waters, though he couldn't appreciate by how much while he was engaged in fighting for his life.

Santos was still roaring out his reckless challenge, but Johnny had a hold on his knife hand, while use of his own pistol was held in check by the savage's grip on his own gun hand. They staggered backwards and forwards, ignoring the hum of passing bullets as the outlaws desperately tried to shoot their way out of the cavern. Dimly he was aware Sarah was still shooting calmly and methodically, presumably at the flashing of discharged weapons for there was no other light. The gunman felt an icy current swirl around his feet and realized the waters were rising faster than he'd ever thought possible. He fell back, rolled to the floor and tried to fling the Indian over his head to break the hold, but Santos was as aware as he that the first to break the hold would be the eventual winner, and he too rolled, jerking hard on his knife arm in a desperate attempt to free himself from the white man's grip.

Johnny dropped back, his head under water for a moment while he made the next manoeuvre. It brought them hard up against Sarah, who, unbalanced by the unexpected collision crashed down on top of them. Neither man could take advantage, but the girl, identifying Johnny's attacker by his slick, bare-skinned torso, fired a shot directly into him. His grip failed, but before the gunman could take his advantage a veritable wall of water hit them. The Indian disappeared into the darkness and Johnny could do no more than grab hold of the girl before they too were swept off their feet.

The water swirled again in an unnerving whorl that sucked hungrily at what little grip they could find on the rocks, and suddenly the pair were flung free into the yawning gap of the entrance shaft. The water in this side chamber was calmer, still enough for Johnny to catch hold of the guide rope and haul himself and Sarah well into the lee of the current.

'Quick,' he cried anxiously, 'the water's rising fast.' Sarah had lost hold of her rifle and showed signs of searching for it until he jerked her savagely back. 'Leave it,' he commanded and began to encourage her up the passage, now awash with icy water that was rapidly rising towards their waists.

A gurgling roar ahead alerted them to the onset of yet another danger. 'Hang on,' Johnny cried out in desperation when he felt the weight of water beginning to suck at his feet. He realized water was being siphoned down one of the side channels, creating a fiercely running current that threatened to take them with it. He roared his defiance to the elements and set his back against the opposite wall of the passage, hauling the girl after him by main force. She, so much lighter, could barely maintain her footing at all, and when she slid, it took all his strength to hold her.

A loud pop signified the moment when the side tunnel filled, and a backlash of icy water exploded back out of the unseen maw, catching them in a torrent of swirling water that finally took them both off their feet. Johnny still maintained a tenuous hold on the guide rope, but even that fragile link to safety looked likely to be torn from his grasp as the waters tossed them to and fro.

Sarah was the first to set her feet to the floor again. One of her hands was tangled in Johnny's battered shirt, a grip that had strengthened every time the sodden material took another turn around her wrist, and she set herself to take his weight until his skittering feet could find their own grip. Johnny's mind was beginning to swirl as fast as the deadly currents that tried again and again to overturn them and, despite his hold on the guide rope, it took him several seconds to decide which direction they should take.

They staggered on, the water lapping higher, but no

longer driven by the same vicious currents. Johnny was vaguely aware that there were at least some of the outlaws not so far behind, themselves struggling to escape from a watery grave. He touched the gun in its holster, where some last instinct had contrived to stow it, but it was no more than a gesture. In the circumstances he was as little prepared to stop their escape as they would be to prevent his, though that situation was bound to change once they reached open ground.

The tunnel shelved rapidly, and suddenly the cold and drenched pair were lurching through the shallows, still holding on to one another, while Johnny's hand remained firm on the guiding rope. A dozen steps, each higher than the last, and their feet were on dry land, though the waters could still be heard seeping up behind them. Sarah gave a gasp of joy and would have collapsed in utter exhaustion if Johnny hadn't urged her on.

'We've got to reach the entrance first,' he told her, his words slurred by the same sense of weariness. He didn't know what awaited them there; the remainder of the gang might be gathered around the shaft that led to safety or, as he hoped, more likely not. They would know nothing of events underground, were more probably sheltering from the storm if it still raged on. In any case, unless the guards were close enough to recognize a face, anyone exiting the cave would automatically be assumed to be friendly so long as none of the outlaws escaped before them. He listened in the darkness, his dragging footsteps matched by his companion. There were cries further back down the cave, whether of encouragement or despair he couldn't tell, but far enough behind not to worry him unduly.

A slim sliver of pale light appeared ahead, spreading

hope through their tired, numb bodies. The dim illumination grew rapidly while they staggered towards it, the icy cold biting into their flesh and slowing their responses. The light was still barely sufficient to see clearly, even close to the shaft that led almost vertically towards the surface, but a tell-tale stream of water staining the wet rocky surfaces suggested the rain was still falling outside, though no longer with the same mind-numbing intensity as when they'd first entered.

'Stay here,' Johnny whispered, holding Sarah by her shoulders. He could see no more than the dim outline of her head, her hair slicked close by the drenching water, but he tipped his head to kiss her gently on the mouth. Then, taking a hold on the rough-hewn pegs of rock that marked the upward path, he pulled himself up slowly, quietly as he was able, knowing that at least one of the outlaws had been on guard when they entered. He drew his pistol and surged through the entrance into the open. Something hard smacked down on his wrist and the gun slipped from his grasp, his numbed and useless fingers unable to maintain their hold.

'Here's one of those murdering rascals,' howled an oddly familiar voice. Then someone hooked the legs out from under him and he crashed to the ground, only vaguely aware that someone else was emerging from the cave.

'Barney, no! It's me, Sarah.' The clearly feminine tones stayed the hands of those who would have tossed her, too, to the ground, while the old ranch-hand whistled through his teeth.

'Miss Sarah,' he began.

Sarah ignored his overtures and instead dropped to her

knees beside Johnny's prone and motionless figure. He groaned and made to get up while she thrust her shoulders under his arm to aid him. His wrist hurt and his mind was still awash with memories of their desperate flight through the cave, but he understood enough to realize the posse had arrived at last.

'What happened down there?'

A tall, slim figure appeared to be in charge, and Johnny gave a concise account of events as he saw them, ending with a plea for the posse to be careful.

'There are some outlaws still alive down there. They're armed and may be dangerous.'

'What about the gold?' A plump man, rather pasty in complexion, broke in. Johnny assumed he had something to do with the bank.

'It's down there too. Under water. There's some real bad currents that may have scattered it, but gold's too heavy to travel far. When the waters recede you ought to be able to recover most of it. In fact, there's some loaded on the wagon already.'

# CHAPTER FOURTEEN

# END OF THE RAINBOW

The rain stopped and Johnny looked up as a watery sun peeped through the rapidly dissipating clouds, spreading its golden rays around the waterlogged ground. Colours swirled out of the damp sky and gathered in a rainbow with magical rapidity. He hooked an arm around Sarah's waist and pulled her close, muttering under his breath when he realized just how much water was still dripping off her cold and sodden form.

'Damn it, Barney,' he began, 'we've got to get Sarah dried out before she takes a chill.'

'You too, for that matter,' returned the old ranch-hand sympathetically. 'No problem, though. I brought the buckboard back with me; easier than riding in my condition.' He pointed apologetically towards the bandages that swathed his right leg. 'The colonel always insisted in storing some blankets under the seat. Wrap 'em around you and light out for the line hut. You've stored your kit out there and Sarah will just have to filch whatever she can from you.'

'Thanks, Barney. We'll be back soon as we can,' Sarah broke in, impatiently pulling Johnny away from the group waiting around the cave's entrance for the surviving gang members to emerge.

'We're of no use here,' she told him firmly. 'There are more than enough men here to deal with the outlaws, and you'll catch your death in those wet clothes.'

Johnny reluctantly nodded his acceptance and followed her lead. They began to clamber through the boulders, while the sunlight lit up her figure, gleaming on the sodden clothes that clung lovingly to her form. For a moment desire struggled to take hold of his deadened senses, but his own clothes were as sodden as hers, and when they tumbled on to the trail proper, the numbing, icy wind bit into his vitals, leaving his hunger for the girl stillborn. A couple of men guarded the old farm wagon and its cargo of captured outlaws, and they were able to direct the waterlogged pair towards Barney's buckboard.

Sarah took the lead and hauled out the blankets. 'Strip,' she told him and with barely a glance around to check that they were out of sight, began to put her own words into practice.

It was a second or two before Johnny's exhausted mind could take in what Sarah meant, and by that time it was too late to turn away. Once she'd discarded her shirt, she peeled off her shift, seeming not to notice that in doing so she'd bared herself in front of him. He watched, mesmerized, his numb and awkward fingers attempting to unfasten his own shirt.

She was staring at him too, he realized. Stock still, bare to the waist, and staring. He looked down and realized what she'd seen. Blood was staining the side of his shirt.

The water had washed it away, but once the rain had stopped the bleeding was obvious. Next moment she was at his side, easing the shirt off his torso, oblivious to her own nudity in her concern.

The knife had sliced into his side, run down his ribs, and carved open the flesh from breast to waist. Blood was welling up all down the wound, but nowhere was it deep enough to affect any vital organ. Nevertheless, he realized he'd lost a lot of blood; no wonder he felt groggy.

'I'll bandage you up properly,' Sarah informed him tenderly, 'at the line hut. There'll be emergency medical stores there. Let's get these off before you catch a chill.' These were his torn and battered work trousers, and working swiftly, she had him stark naked and wrapped in a blanket before he had time to object. A moment later she too was peeling off the remainder of her clothes. A fleeting glimpse of coarse, slicked down hair the same colour as her head, was curtailed as quickly when she snuggled into the warmth of a blanket herself.

Sarah drove the horses fast, laughing when he buckled the leather gun belt around his waist over the blanket, a laugh that melted into concern when he winced at the pain from his wound while he cinched up the tooled leather. Funny how the wound should hurt so much now he was aware of it!

'No sense in taking chances,' he told her, and drew another blanket around his shoulders.

Once they arrived at the tiny cabin, Sarah slipped off the buckboard and ran lightly to the door. 'Never mind the horses,' she told him, and disappeared inside.

Habit is a fine thing. It never occurred to Johnny that he should leave the horses. These were animals you might have to rely on in rough country, and it had been ingrained in him over the years that their needs came first. Despite his wounds, his practised hands made short work of unharnessing the pair and leading them around to the corral, where he left them to run free.

Exhaustion and the effects of his injuries had let his defences down. He should have known someone had beat them to the line hut. The signs were all around, even down to the extra horse in the corral. He drew his pistol and approached the cabin with care.

Randy Nolan lounged out of the doorway. Sarah was held fast in front of him, shielding the vicious outlaw from the gunman's aim. Randy's own gun was in his holster, but he held a knife to the girl's throat.

'Put your gun up.' Nolan's nasal whine seemed harsher than ever.

'Leave her,' Johnny looked for an opening while he spoke and continued to hold the gun steady on its target. 'It's me you want, not the girl.'

'I won't ask you nicely again,' the outlaw warned. The knife flashed in a short arc, dipping to slice open a section of the blanket, which dropped away to reveal one full breast and Johnny cursed angrily when the outlaw reached around with his free hand to caress it. 'It would be a pity to mark such a beauty,' the outlaw continued, squeezing hard enough to draw a squeal of fear from the girl. Her captor laughed with evil intensity and waved the knife suggestively.

Johnny paled visibly and held his arms wide, prepared to drop his pistol rather than risk Sarah's life. It wouldn't save her in the long run, nor him either, but he couldn't risk a shot while she was held so close.

'Place the gun back in its holster carefully,' invited Nolan with a baying laugh, while he subjected Sarah to another lewd caress that made her shudder afresh with distaste.

'They tell me you're good with a gun,' he continued in conversational tone. 'So this seems like a good time to discover who's the faster, you or me.' He laughed again with manic intensity. 'Right now!' The outlaw raised his voice to rap out the strident command.

Johnny could hardly believe his ears. Surely the man wasn't issuing a challenge? Not when he'd already got the drop on him. He holstered the gun and stood straight, half expecting to be shot where he stood.

Once Johnny had obeyed his command and holstered his pistol, Nolan flung the girl to the ground with a contemptuous shrug. He laughed again when she brushed the blankets down to cover her legs, exposed by the fall, but his eyes never left the tall figure of his adversary.

Johnny started forward, but the outlaw stopped him with a gesture. 'The girl will be my prize,' he told the gunman. 'Nice of her to get undressed ready.' He stepped confidently out of the shadowed doorway.

Nolan was right to feel confident. Johnny began to consider the situation: his sight was fuzzy, his head was spinning, and in any case, competent though he was with a gun, he'd never considered himself a fast draw expert.

He stared at the man who was going to kill him, saw him lean forward to pick up a small rock and hold it up. Johnny felt as though he was going to collapse at any minute, but made one last effort to roll back the mists of exhaustion that threatened to overwhelm him.

'I'll drop this rock and we'll draw when it reaches the ground.' Nolan ground out the rules, smiling wolfishly when he saw how weak his opponent was.

Johnny ignored these signs of premature celebration and concentrated on making his final effort. The mists of exhaustion rolled back and, for the moment at least, he regained the icy-calm demeanour of a man ready to fight for his life. His numbed and painful fingers hooked into claws at his side, ready to go for his gun as soon as the stone hit the ground. Nolan was a dead man, even if he, himself, had to die taking him.

The rock was thrown, and Nolan, a cheat and liar to the end, immediately sought to take advantage. His hand blurred into the motions of the fast draw, designed to take his opponent before he'd even reacted. But Johnny had fought with such men before; he'd seen the move reflected in Nolan's eyes and his own smoothly practised draw was already under way.

Two guns slid from their holsters in unison, levelled and fired simultaneously. Only one would fire again! Johnny staggered, his legs gave way and he dropped with a thud, echoed by Sarah's shriek of despair. He'd been hit, bad enough to knock him off his feet, but he didn't know where. Didn't matter, only killing Nolan mattered. The outlaw was slumped helplessly against the cabin wall, staining the rough hewn timber with his life blood while he slithered slowly to the floor. Johnny fired once again to make sure, drilling his shell into the same heart his first shot had stopped.

Barney found the pair of them several hours later, sleeping peacefully under a pile of fresh, warm blankets. Despite her bleak mood and shaking hands, Johnny's wounds had been dressed while Sarah could still keep her eyes open, and then they'd fallen into the bed together, too exhausted by the day's events to do any more than fall asleep in each other's arms.